CURSE OF THE WULFEN

CURSE OF THE WULFEN

DAVID ANNANDALE

BLACK LIBRARY

For Margaux. All gifts, always.

A BLACK LIBRARY PUBLICATION

First published in Great Britain in 2016 by
Black Library,
Games Workshop Ltd.,
Willow Road,
Nottingham, NG7 2WS, UK.

10 9 8 7 6 5 4 3 2 1

Produced by Games Workshop in Nottingham.

UK ISBN 13: 978 1 78496 087 2
Product Code: 60040181188

See Black Library on the internet at

blacklibrary.com

Find out more about Games Workshop
and the world of Warhammer 40,000 at

games-workshop.com

Printed in China

It is the 41st millennium. For more than a hundred centuries the Emperor has sat immobile on the Golden Throne of Earth. He is the master of mankind by the will of the gods, and master of a million worlds by the might of his inexhaustible armies. He is a rotting carcass writhing invisibly with power from the Dark Age of Technology. He is the Carrion Lord of the Imperium for whom a thousand souls are sacrificed every day, so that he may never truly die.

Yet even in his deathless state, the Emperor continues his eternal vigilance. Mighty battlefleets cross the daemon-infested miasma of the warp, the only route between distant stars, their way lit by the Astronomican, the psychic manifestation of the Emperor's will. Vast armies give battle in His name on uncounted worlds. Greatest amongst his soldiers are the Adeptus Astartes, the Space Marines, bioengineered super-warriors. Their comrades in arms are legion: the Astra Militarum and countless planetary defence forces, the ever-vigilant Inquisition and the tech-priests of the Adeptus Mechanicus to name only a few. But for all their multitudes, they are barely enough to hold off the ever-present threat from aliens, heretics, mutants – and worse.

To be a man in such times is to be one amongst untold billions. It is to live in the cruellest and most bloody regime imaginable. These are the tales of those times. Forget the power of technology and science, for so much has been forgotten, never to be re-learned. Forget the promise of progress and understanding, for in the grim dark future there is only war. There is no peace amongst the stars, only an eternity of carnage and slaughter, and the laughter of thirsting gods.

PROLOGUE

They met in the dark of the mountain's roots. Here the night of stone was endless. It was not silent, for things of fur and fang and steel prowled, growling warnings to each other. It was not empty, for within it lay the tombs of legends. The tombs were unquiet. The legends they enclosed were granted only a provisional death. These sagas had not ended. One was ten thousand years old, and its thread carried on.

Three warriors met in the dark, in the tombs. When they saw each other, they were startled. When they saw where they had come to, they were disturbed.

The warrior whose mane and beard were as coarse and grey as a wolf's pelt spoke first. 'Brothers,' Harald Deathwolf said, 'you are well met. I did not expect your company.'

'Nor I,' said Krom Dragongaze. Even in the gloom, his eyes glittered with dark light.

'Nor I,' Ulrik the Slayer echoed. The ancient of the Chapter shook his head. His hair was as white as his gaze was dark. His eyes were shadows that watched and judged. He pointed at the vault door by which they stood. 'There is a purpose in this,' he said.

'The purpose is not mine,' said Harald. 'I did not intend to come here.' He looked at the name inscribed over the door, and was uneasy.

'You did not choose to come to the vaults?' the Slayer asked.

'I did,' said Harald. 'But with no clear design. That is...' he hesitated.

'You walked as if in a trance,' Dragongaze said.

'Yes.'

'So we all did,' said the Slayer. 'But not as we believed.'

'No.' Harald tried to see the last few hours clearly, but it was as if he had only just awakened, a sensation itself almost unknown to him in his centuries as a Space Marine. He had been conscious, yet his perception had narrowed to nothing except his next footstep. He had moved through tunnels and shafts, down and down and down, deeper and deeper into the dark, into the night of stone. 'I had a destination,' he said. 'Though I did not know why I went. The need to be there was absolute.' He could not look away from the inscription. 'My destination was not here.'

'You thought to stand before Bjorn the Fell-Handed,' Dragongaze said.

'I did.'

'And yet we are here,' said the Slayer. The Wolf Priest rested a gauntlet against the vault door, gently, as if not to wake the legend inside. 'We marched to one goal, and arrived at another. This is a powerful omen, brothers. We must take heed.'

'An omen of what?' said Dragongaze.

'I will think upon it,' the Slayer said. 'This much is clear. Something is coming. The force of our compulsion speaks to its magnitude. And when the event arrives, we three must be mindful of the roles we will have to play.'

'It is a warning,' Harald said. 'An omen of doom. How can it be otherwise? We sought Bjorn, but we came here.'

The other two said nothing. They all gazed at the inscription. They stared at the runes of warning and the name of the mad legend, and felt a shadow deeper yet than the night of stone fall over their souls.

Beyond me lies a restless sleep, said the door. *Beyond me lies the madness of wrath.*

Murderfang.

The future stalked towards them, jaws agape.

PART 1:
THE RETURN

CHAPTER 1

The Dooms on Nurades

'The sky is blue today, governor.'

Andras Elsener, Lord Governor of Nurades, looked up from the sea of parchment and data-slates on the vast iron table before him. Everything was a priority, and everything had to be decided *now*. And this was merely what he had to wade through for the next hour. It was early in the day yet. The interruption was welcome, though he knew he would pay for the break in his concentration later.

Klein, his major-domo, stood at the chamber window. Elsener's quarters were high in the spire of Hive Genos. The view from his office looked out across the spires of the hive from a point that was frequently, although not always, a little below cloud cover. Sometimes Elsener could see many kilometres of the sprawl of the hive. Sometimes he saw nothing but a choking, industrial grey-brown. Twice in his life he had witnessed the weak disc of the sun visible through unusually thin clouds.

He had never seen a blue sky.

Elsener approached the window in wary awe. Klein seemed just as uneasy. He was about to open the door to the balcony but Elsener stopped him.

'No,' said the governor. 'Wait.'

The sky was clear. The blue was startling. It was searing. As Elsener watched, the last of the cloud cover peeled away like burning paper. The blue became brighter and brighter, though Elsener could not see the sun. The colour became painful. Elsener squinted. Klein shielded his eyes.

And then, though the colour still grew more intense, it also became darker. Blue became violet.

'The Emperor save us,' Elsener muttered.

Violet turned to a dark, grimy crimson. The colour of rotting blood stabbed at the back of Elsener's eyes. He could not look away. At the height of the searing, the sky ignited. Flames burst across the firmament. They were huge, arcing, roiling, as if Nurades had been pitched into a molten cauldron. The sky burned all the colours of the spectrum at once, destroying them with fury. As they died, the colours gave birth to other things, things that existed instead of colours, things that bled the eyes and tore at the mind.

The ground heaved. The central spire of Genos swayed back and forth. Narrower towers collapsed. But new spires rose, piercing up through the layers of the hive, thrusting towards the sky like monstrous daggers, and they were towers of bone.

Elsener saw dots appear in the sky. They fell – dark, tumbling, blazing orbs. Closer, and he saw they were skulls. They were a laughing, screaming hail. Jaws agape, they smashed onto the roofs and walkways and roads. They shattered on Elsener's balcony. Where each landed, its fire spread. It grew taller. It took on a shape. Now it had arms, legs. Now a head. Horns.

Muscle and sinew and blood-red flesh. It carried a sword.

Elsener cried out and hurled himself away from the window. He must not look. He must not see. Already he could feel his brain squirming as if it would change into an animal inside his skull.

Klein shrieked. He clawed at his face hard enough to tear open his cheeks. He clutched at his ragged flaps of skin, then ran at the governor, howling and drooling. Elsener drew his personal laspistol and shot the major-domo through the neck.

Then he ran. He did not look back, not even when the window smashed, and a snarling abomination called out to him in a voice of rattling bone. He knew what would happen if he looked. Perhaps he would die in the next few seconds, but if he did not look, he might yet retain his soul.

He prayed to the Emperor as he charged through the door and down the halls of his residence. He prayed the Father of Mankind would grant that he reached the astropathic choir in time. He prayed someone would hear Nurades' cry for help.

The next time Lord Governor Andras Elsener dared to look at the sky, it was weeks later, and he saw the cry answered.

He saw salvation slash through sky with bloody claws.

In the strategium overlooking the bridge of the strike cruiser *Alpha Fang*, the great predator leaned over a hololithic map of Nurades. A mantle of troll hide was draped over his armour, a trophy made of the prey itself. His gestures suggested contained force. At any moment, they could turn into the strike of a hunter. And moment by moment, he chose restraint. His calm was that of a wolf that had already chosen when and how to attack.

Harald Deathwolf pointed to the sigil for Hive Predomitus.

'We begin there,' he said. The hive was located at the base of a high mountain chain dividing the Lacertus Peninsula from the rest of the continent. 'We break the daemons' hold.' He moved his hand south-west, passing over Hive Genos. 'And push them into the sea.'

Canis Wolfborn looked from the map to the oculus. It showed the void riven by the mad flares of the warp storm, and the planet turning in agony. The atmosphere quivered like maggots. The Deathwolf champion grunted. 'Saving that?'

The huge warrior was more restless than Harald. His mane and beard were a lighter shade and longer, more unruly. If Harald was the wolf assured of closing its jaws on its prey, the Feral Knight was the beast barely held back. The bridge was not his natural domain. He belonged in the field, unleashed and roaring.

'Mistress of the vox,' Harald called without looking up from the map. 'Any traffic planetside?'

'Some, lord,' Giske Ager replied. 'Fragments only. There are brief bursts of coherent data. Orders perhaps. There are many cries.'

Harald nodded. He addressed the assembled Wolf Guard, not just Canis. The Deathwolf huscarls varied widely in age. But whether they counted themselves among the Riders of Morkai, the Thunderclaws or the Redhowl Hunters, they were all riders of wolves, and there was a kinship in their countenance – a narrowed, farseeing, predatory gaze.

'We have answered a plea for help,' Harald said. 'We have not come to enact Exterminatus. This planet will not be lost. I will see it returned to the embrace of the Allfather.'

'A hunt then,' said Vygar Helmfang.

'A great one.'

'Good.' Canis growled in satisfaction and anticipation. His question, Harald understood, had not been an expression of doubt in the mission. Canis wanted reassurance that he would not be cheated of prey by cyclonic torpedoes.

The assembled Wolf Guard also sounded pleased with Harald's deployment strategy. The Lacertus Peninsula was the most densely populated and industrially active region of Nurades. When the Space Wolves took it, they would hold the key to the rest of the world.

Harald wondered if it might also unlock something else. The encounter before Murderfang's vault troubled him. He was waiting for whatever event it heralded to make itself manifest. He did not know if the plight of Nurades meant more than it appeared, but there were unusual circumstances. From what had been gathered from the astropathic shriek that had reached Fenris, the coming of the warp storm had been extremely sudden. A matter of seconds. There was something about that arrival that did not seem like the result of the vagaries of the warp and a chance weakness in the materium.

Harald sensed a larger game behind the incursion. He could not guess what it was, nor what, if anything, it portended for the Space Wolves.

No matter, he tried to tell himself. His Great Company would stamp out the daemonic taint, and end the game before it began.

The Deathwolves fell upon the daemonic hordes much as the warp-spawn had attacked the people of Nurades – with sudden, lightning violence.

The drop pods came first, streaking through the tormented sky in a cluster towards the plain between the mountains and the gates of Hive Predomitus. The Stormwolf gunships followed in their con-trails. They hammered the landing site with twin-linked lascannon and heavy bolter fire, annihilating daemonkind in the vicinity.

The flanks of the pods slammed down and the Space Wolves stormed out. Grey Hunters howled their eagerness for war. Their helms bore totemic skulls and tails. Some were fashioned into snarling lupine form. They thundered away, in pack after pack. They hurled frag grenades ahead of them, then followed up the blasts with a stream of bolter fire. Monstrosities disintegrated. The Death-wolves pushed the enemy further back, allowing the gunships to land. Caught in the heat of first blood, the Grey Hunters would have followed their instincts to charge on if their pack leaders had not held them back long enough for the rest of their brothers to disembark.

The wait was a short one. Harald's full company launched a blistering assault on the enemy within seconds of having their boots on the ground.

Before the gates of Predomitus, a mass of horned, scarlet-scaled abominations rioted.

'Swordlings of Khorne.' Canis spat his contempt. His breath came in low growls.

'They have not been idle,' Harald said.

In the midst of the daemons rose tall hills of blackened skulls. Millions of Nuradeans had been sacrificed to Khorne, but the hunger of the god and his servants was unending. From the open gates of the city, the daemons dragged thousands upon thousands of howling victims.

'I can see the hills growing,' Canis said. His face was dark with horrified fury.

'So vast a slaughter,' Harald growled. 'Let our answer be more terrible still.'

The Stormwolf squadrons took to the air, pounding the warpspawn with guns. Lasbeams and shells burned daemons and blew them apart. They cut a seared, smoking furrow through the mass of wyrdflesh.

'The hunt is on, brothers!' Harald called. His roar was a clarion call to war, and Grey Hunters and Wolf Guard answered with a roar of their own. The battle cry thundered from the throats of men and beasts, and the thunderwolf cavalry led the charge into the furrow. Harald was at the front atop Icetooth, with Canis at his shoulder, as the immense Fangir shook the earth as he loped forward. Alongside the cavalry sped the Huntbrothers and the Frostrunners, Fenrisian wolves, some pure animal, others cybernetic hybrids, all of them monsters, flesh with strength of steel and steel with the wrath of flesh.

The cavalry slammed into their lines with the force of a nova cannon. Tens of thousands of daemons massed on the plain. They were hatred embodied. But they fell back, trampled into oblivion by the wolves, blasted apart by bolter fire. Harald felt the exultant ferocity of war flood his veins. The vastness of the enemy army meant nothing except a near-inexhaustible supply of prey. His view turned from the hills of bodies and the burning towers of Predomitus to the horrors that surged, grasping for him. He swung his right arm out. The storm shield on his forearm smashed horns and skulls. He relished the impact. The jar was solid, crunching. He fired his bolt pistol as he swung. Wyrdflesh erupted before him. With his left hand, he wielded the frost axe Glacius. Its huge, wedge-shaped blade was a single crystal shard. It glinted the blue of razored cold. The edge was as long as Harald's arm. Daemonic flesh and muscle and bone ruptured at its strike.

Moments into the charge, Harald's senses were filled with the stench of roiling smoke and spraying ichor. Daemons howled with unnatural voices. The air shook with the clash of rages.

The swordlings tried to surround the charge and bring the cavalry down in a tide of blood. No matter how many of them rushed in, they could not stop the Deathwolves' momentum, although they exacted a toll. Harald heard the agonised snarls of a thunderwolf and the growls of Rangvald, its rider. He heard the crash as Wolf Guard and beast hit the ground under a mass of clawing, slashing daemons. There was an explosion of bolter fire as the brothers nearby sought to blast the swordlings away from the fallen rider.

'Ride on, brothers,' Rangvald shouted, fighting to the last.

And they did. The charge could not slow for anyone. Its success against such a vast horde depended on relentless violence and speed. With each fallen brother, the wrath of the Space Wolves and the thunderwolves grew, and they smashed the daemons with ever-greater ferocity. Harald saw only red – the red of the abominated flesh, the red of flame, and the red of his anger. Icetooth crushed daemons in his jaws. He smashed them to nothing beneath his enormous claws.

At Harald's shoulder, Canis' snarls were expressions of wrath and laughter. He swept his huge wolf claws back and forth, embracing the enemy with destruction. Every blade was as long as a gladius. Harald glanced to the right in time to see Canis slash a daemon's spine into sections with a single swipe.

'A good kill, brother!' Harald called.

The champion grinned, his yellow eyes blazing. He shouted something back, but all Harald heard was an inarticulate snarl. Canis was already deep into primal ferocity. He was in the realm of the beast now.

It would be easy to join him. Already Harald growled with triumph at each of Icetooth's kills. They were as one alpha predator in the field of battle. The bloody charge was exhilarating. The smoky wind blew back Harald's hair and beard. The beat of his hearts matched the pounding of Icetooth's paws. The thundering anger of bolters, wolves and men carried him forward. Even the stench of ichor, a miasma both clutching and jagged, was a goad.

The call of absolute frenzy was strong. He held back, though. Not much, but just enough to hold on to his awareness of the wider field of battle.

The Deathwolves battered their way forward to victory and slaughter. The thunderwolf charge blew apart the lines of the Khornate abominations. It reduced hundreds of them to a thick sludge of ichor. The power of the wyrd crackled over them, and the foul liquid did not dissipate. Icetooth's paws splashed through a deepening mire. Their anger could not summon the strength to meet the challenge of the Deathwolves. Without pause, without mercy, Harald cut through the daemons and reached the wall of Predomitus.

He did not lead the charge through the gates. Instead, he turned right along the ramparts, then turned again to smash back down through the horde. At his back, he felt the blasting wind of two gunships. They made low passes before the gates, hammering the ground with heavy bolters and lascannons. The gap in the wall became an inferno. Harald looked back to see volcanic destruction, the earth and bodies heaving skyward. Daemons burned as they flew. The horde within the city could not break out. The other Stormwolves flew in from the rear of the lines to meet the advancing cavalry, scything a swath of annihilation as they came.

A daemon leapt high over Icetooth's jaws. It came down directly at Harald, its sword descending to cut his head in two. He brought up the shield and smashed it aside. He finished it off with a bolt shell to the skull. Icetooth seized another abomination by the neck and bit through with a single clamp of his jaws.

Harald seized the moment to look left. In the wake of the cavalry charge, the infantry was advancing, the speed more deliberate but the destruction no less total. The Grey Hunters were still moving towards the gates, cutting an even wider swath. Harald heard their massed war shouts over the cries of the daemons.

Behind the gunships and infantry came the tanks. Predators, Vindicators and Land Raiders in tight formation became a giant grinder, an unstoppable mass of metal and cannon fire. Icetooth ran towards the explosions. Purifying flame pushed back the wyrd-light.

'Riding close!' Canis yelled, coherent again, his voice still guttural. He impaled a swordling through the throat and hurled the creature away to the right, into the blades of its kin. 'Straight to the blasts?' he asked.

Harald could almost believe Canis was ready to pursue the slaughter right into the tank fire.

'Not quite,' he said. But he grinned at his champion. 'Close though.'

He waited until the smoke was choking, shattered stone was raining down on the field, and the concussions were deafening then swerved off to the right, clearing the way for the tanks. The clanking, booming vehicles moved past the cavalry, rolling over the daemons that had been in pursuit.

Canis growled in disappointment. The field before the Thunderwolves was almost empty of daemons.

'We aren't done, brother,' Harald said. 'We're a long way from done.' He turned Icetooth back towards the wall, and they rode a short distance to the flank of the armour. They came around a hill of skulls, and fell upon another horde.

The abominations were in disarray. They could not mount a counter attack. Their numbers worked against them as they tried to respond to the sudden changes in the Deathwolves' vector of destruction. All the thousands in the plain became fodder for the claws of the Space Wolves. The daemons could not attack at once. They hindered each other's movements as Harald triggered conflicting currents of attack. In their rage and frustration, the creatures fell to fighting each other.

The cavalry charge was unrelenting. Hours into the battle, the Deathwolves raced with the same speed and fury as their initial assault. And when at last Harald called a halt, the nature of the plain had changed. The sky overhead remained a storm of dark, mad flame. Smoke rose from the hills of skulls, and blood pooled at their bases. But the cracked earth was barren. The enemy was gone.

Slaughter and victory. So often, they were the same thing. On this day they were. While the gunships continued to pound the gates of Predomitus, Harald regarded the dead land with satisfaction. This much of Nurades was purged.

Beside him, Canis said, 'A good start.' He was hungry for more.

We all are, Harald thought. His blood was up. The annihilation of the enemy in this first encounter, and the imperative to keep up the pressure pushed the concerns of the war's significance to the back of his mind. The plan of a foe was meaningless if the foe was exterminated. And Harald felt the strength of extermination in his hands. He was a predator unleashed, and there was prey on the other side of the walls.

'Yes,' he said to Canis. 'A good start to the hunt. Let us continue.'

The battle for Predomitus took days. Days of unending massacre. In the stages of the purging, the Deathwolves broke though a crush of daemons at the gates, then moved up the primary thoroughfares of the hive. The war was an interior one now. Only rarely did the company emerge into open air, though the pilots of the gunships kept as close to the position of their brothers as possible, strafing the exposed positions of the hive. They blew up towers where the concentration of daemons was so great that the buildings themselves had begun to distort, rockcrete walls turning into scaly flesh.

In the hive, the daemons answered the challenge of the Death-wolves. They poured in from halls and chambers. They crashed through skylights and ventilation shafts. They erupted from the floors of the route. The Great Company cut them down. Harald kept up the speed of the attack, moving almost as quickly as the initial charge. There was no chance of surprise when the battle was continuous, as unbroken as the flow of a burning river of blood.

The Deathwolves moved fast, with the savagery of the beasts they rode. But Harald chose the path of their assault with care. Aboard the *Alpha Fang*, he had studied hololithic schematics of Nurades' hive cities. The frenzy of his hunt was tempered by strategy. He embraced the wolf. He fought as if he were one. *As if* he were one. There was a difference. Never to be forgotten.

Once the gate was taken, Harald began the second stage of the assault on Predomitus. He split his forces to take the cavalry and infantry down the narrower passages, while the tanks moved implacably down the main arteries. The smaller routes were large enough to permit rapid deployment, but not so wide the daemons could mass sufficient numbers together to slow the advance. The daemons took the bait, and Harald exterminated them.

'This is the long charge, brothers,' Harald voxed the Great Company as the Wolf Guard and Grey Hunters slaughtered daemons, rejoined the tanks on the great avenues, then split off to repeat the pattern. 'This is how we will take back Predomitus. Our victory rests on momentum and speed. Depend upon that.'

Canis tore a swordling in half then gestured at the vista of towering walls and branching avenues lying ahead. 'This is a vast hunt,' he said.

Harald switched to a private channel. 'We do not seek a complete purge,' he said. That would be impossible. 'It will be enough to break the daemons' grip.' He pointed up and to the left, where the upper storeys of a spire flashed with lasbeam fire. 'Nurades still has uncorrupted defence forces. We will give them the means to mount their war of reclamation, then move to the next target.' He thought the prospect of an unending, savage advance would please Canis.

He was right. The champion howled as he and Fangir hurled themselves at the next group of daemons.

The course of the war took the Deathwolves deep into the underhive. There the concentration of daemons was immense. And in

the Industrium Sub-terranal, the abominations mounted a challenge to Harald's advance.

The Industrium was a tangle of passages. Machinery was piled
upon machinery in a gloom lit by fiery outgassing, and centuries
of construction and decay had created jumbled layers of manufactoria. The millions of serfs who worked the Industrium were gone,
transformed or dead. Many regions of the steel maze were ruins,
and the dead metal was changing into hungry flesh. But much of the
machinery was still active, gears turning, jaws grinding ore, forges
pouring out molten metal with the mindless persistence of titanic
servitors. The passages here were short, broken, unpredictable.
Machinic walls rumbled towards each other, then parted. Angles
were sharp, and speed was dangerous, difficult, and still necessary.
And here, there were other daemons.

Until now, the Deathwolves had fought only Khornate abominations, howling embodiments of rage. In the Industrium, they
encountered daemons of Tzeentch. Instead of roars, mad laughter echoed down the passageways. Voices intoned sentences that
hovered on the edge of human meaning. The words scratched at
the back of Harald's eyes.

'Silence the tongues of the wyrd!' he yelled, his voice ringing off
the iron walls. The lead Thunderwolves trampled the daemonic, misshapen horrors of glistening pink muscle. They came apart beneath
claws and chainswords. Flesh parted, darkened to the blue of contu-
sions and reformed. The daemons multiplied in their destruction, but
were hammered into oblivion by the bolter fire of the Grey Hunters.

Sudden, inhuman shrieks split the air apart. Airborne daemons,
things that were little more than wings and horns and whiplash
tails, came screaming around the sharp turns, and flew out from
between dark crevasses in the machinery. They were mindless but
agile. They fell upon the Deathwolves, lunging in with their horns
or slashing past with their spiked tails. They came from all directions, attacked and flew off, then came back.

Harald trusted to the predatory instincts of Icetooth to deal with the daemons that scampered forwards on the floor of the Industrium. He kept his focus on the air, drilling bolt shells into the screaming daemons that swooped his way, raising Glacius to cleave their undersides open if they got by his barrage.

The struggle was composed of moments as disjointed as the space of the Industrium. A war of reckless speed. The pistoning, clanking, smoke-spewing masses of machinery rising hundreds of metres on either side. The ceiling just above Harald's head one moment, invisible in the dark heights the next. No way to prepare for each jagged intersection – nothing for it but to race deep into the whirring saw blades of war. The Deathwolves and the screamers streaking past and through each other, ichor and blood a thick spray in the gloom. The shrieks of the abominations entwined with chants and laughter. The howls of the thunderwolves and snarls of their riders cut though the foul braiding of Chaos with the purity of savagery. War turned into a blur of slashing lethality.

In the depths of the Industrium's maze, Harald became aware of a stronger presence. The attacks of the screamers were too precise for mindless daemons. They were directed by a powerful will. Its whisper travelled through the clamour of battle, slithering worm-like through the interstices of cackle and growl and roar. It spoke to the Deathwolves. It would not be ignored.

Another attack, more insidious, more dangerous.

Slithertwyst welcomes you. Slithertwyst has been waiting. You have been long in coming. Will you make the path interesting? Chains and ropes, manacles and webs, such rattling and struggling and twisting and twisting and twisting. Do you see? You do not see. Hurry, playthings. Hurry and see.

Hissing with secrets, dark with knowledge.

'Shut out the lies!' Harald called to his riders.

But in his heart, he dreaded that somewhere in the daemon's blandishments was a truth more corrosive than any lie.

Shut out Slithertwyst? Silence Slithertwyst? Will you silence fate? Will you shut out your days and ways to come?

On the right, dying metal shrieked. A chain of collapses smothered explosions and a stream of incandescent gas flashed overhead. Harald hunched beneath it. On instinct he turned towards the falling wall. Millions of tonnes of metal toppled towards the Deathwolves. Disintegrating machinery threw out spinning shrapnel. The collapse stretched ahead and behind the cavalry. There was no evading the avalanche – Harald raced towards the certainty of crushing oblivion and it parted before him, a conglomeration with the mass of a hundred Stormwolves tearing to either side like a shredded curtain.

Harald and Canis rode head-on at the daemon that whispered in their souls. Slithertwyst stood astride a screamer. The herald of Tzeentch was a being of limbs and horns and teeth, a huge pink abomination draped in robes of shifting, oily blue. Things sprouted from its body that changed from tentacles to horns from moment to moment. It raised a twisted blade, laughing and whispering at the same time, three more arms spreading wide in welcome to the Space Wolves.

Harald urged Icetooth into a leap. The thunderwolf sailed upwards and came down on the head of the winged daemon, slamming it to the ground. The herald leapt from its wounded steed and flailed at Harald's storm shield with claws and tentacles. The power of the wyrd was in its strength. It hit with serpentine speed and the force of a battering ram, forcing Harald and Icetooth back. The other daemon rose to the aid of its master, and Canis and Fangir fell upon it. Canis slashed the winged monster with his wolf claws, his attack as ferocious as Fangir's, while Harald blocked Slithertwyst's blade thrust with Glacius and fired a sustained volley with his bolt pistol into the daemon's face.

The mass-reactive shells exploded inside its skull. The herald was not a thing of true flesh, but here on Nurades it had a physical reality, and the blasts blew its head into two halves. They hung, deflated sacks of flesh, to either side of the body. The claws scrabbled blindly for Harald, and Icetooth snarled in pain and rage as they dug furrows into his hide. The thunderwolf leapt again, away from the screamer as Slithertwyst's shredded body crashed into the wreckage of burning machinery. The cavalry attacked the thrashing daemon with chainswords and bolt pistols, shattering its body even further. Eldritch flame erupted from where Slithertwyst had fallen. There was a sudden blast, and a foul wind, strong as a hurricane howled through the ruins to batter the Deathwolves.

As they rode through the collapse to the next open passage, Canis said, 'Easy prey.'

The champion was right. They had hit Slithertwyst hard, but Harald had not expected the battle to be so brief.

'Too easy, do you think?' he asked.

'No,' Canis grinned. 'Just poor prey. At least they are many.'

Harald glanced back. The glow of the daemonic fire was fading, the wind dropping. He saw no hint of a resurrection. The whispers had stopped. But for a moment, in the curls of the wind, he thought he heard serpentine laughter.

Canis was satisfied to view the daemons as outmatched, but Harald was not. 'Yet the wyrd is strong on this world,' he said.

Canis didn't answer. He was riding towards his next kill, shouting with feral eagerness.

Doubt gnawed at the edges of Harald's war lust. *There is something I am not seeing.*

Ahead, a swarm of the pink daemons squeezed through a narrow passage. There was no time to contemplate the nature of the herald's demise. The slaughter called, and could not be ignored.

Onwards, then, and onwards, the Deathwolves forever charging, forever cutting through daemonic bodies, ending laughter and chants, purifying every corner they passed in the Industrium's maze.

Taking back Predomitus.

At last, the Deathwolves came through the hive. Their assault, a single run lasting many days, left behind a swath of scoured ruins. The war for the hive was not over, but the balance had tipped towards the mortal defenders. The abomination and the heretic were being burned from Predomitus, and the work would go on until none remained, even if every spire of the city was toppled in the process.

The tide had turned. Harald's cavalry, joined by the heavy armour and the gunships, moved on. Before them, the land between Predomitus and Genos seethed with daemons. They came down from the higher ground, a frothing wave of monstrosity.

'All kinds of filth,' said Canis.

Harald nodded. The alliance of daemons had been hidden by the initial encounter with the swordlings. The presence of the Tzeentchian daemons in the Industrium Sub-terranal had been an ill omen. Now it was confirmed. Wrath and change and plague and excess rampaged over the tortured earth of Nurades. All the shades of the Ruinous Powers were united. 'This does not happen without great cause,' Harald said.

'They want this world badly,' Canis said.

'Do they?' Harald wondered. He thought about the relative ease of Slithertwyst's defeat again. He shook off the speculation. Whatever the purpose of Chaos, the Space Wolves were here to end it.

Though he and his brothers had just come through an exhausting campaign, he rose on Icetooth's back as if fresh to the battlefield, Glacius held high.

'Brothers!' he called. 'Let us hunt again!'

The Emperor's predators tore over the land to slake their thirst for war.

Weeks, then. After Predomitus, weeks of battle across the length of the Lacertus Peninsula. Always forwards, never retreating, cutting through daemons, and pushing them towards the sea, taking back the world they had stolen. The grind of battle in the hive now expanded to an entire region, with kilometres gained each day, but so many more to go, and an entire world infested.

Harald did not look towards an end of the campaign. He concerned himself with the victory of the moment, and of the steps necessary to reach the end. In seeking to counter his strategy, the daemons aided him. They brought more and more of their forces to bear against the Deathwolves, and so they hurried their extermination.

Forty days after the siege of Predomitus, the Deathwolves crested a ridge and caught their first glimpse of the sea, still hundreds of kilometres away. Below, the land dropped away gradually into an arid, rolling plain. It was a cauldron of daemons. Harald paused. He looked upon a heaving mass of beings, a nightmare drawn for the darkest sagas.

'A fine hunt,' Canis said. His face and beard were matted with ichor, and his armour was scored with burns and the marks of other-worldly blades. 'Glorious.' He looked towards the daemonic legions, his hunger for battle as strong as ever.

'Can a hunt be too glorious?' Harald said.

Canis turned to him in disbelief. After a long moment, he laughed, as if deciding Harald was joking. 'Never,' Canis said.

At the moment the champion's laughter ended, Harald thought he heard the echo of another, sibilant voice. Harald glanced around. Slithertwyst's final mockery haunted him.

Every day of the campaign, he watched for the daemon's return. In the corner of his left eye, he saw a dark pink movement. He looked. There was nothing there.

'What did you hear?' Canis asked.

'I thought I heard the daemon who taunted us in Predomitus.'

Canis looked puzzled once more. 'That cannot be. We banished it. Tore it apart.'

Yet it laughed. 'And why Nurades?' he said, finally asking the question out loud. 'What is the meaning of this incursion?'

'Its meaning?' Canis said. 'What does it matter? The daemons' purpose dies with them.'

Does it? It must.

Yet it laughed.

He shook his head. 'You're right, Wolfborn,' he said, trying to convince himself. 'Deathwolves!' he voxed to the company. 'We push to the sea! Leave only death in our wake!'

They poured down the slope. A storm of claws and guns descended on the daemons.

Harald was unable to savour the taste of the victories as they came. The questions gave him no peace. Even in the thick of battle, as he roared and slew, they lingered, as insistent as they were half-formed.

Onward. Forwards. Weeks of war. Weeks of slaughter. The beasts forever unleashed, claws and fangs ripping the unholy foe apart. The infinity of the enemy merely an infinity of prey.

Canis exulted.

Harald doubted.

On and on. Endless.

Until there was an end.

The Lacertus Peninsula came to an abrupt halt. The restless sea hurled itself against sheer basalt cliffs hundreds of metres high. Caught in the tormented energy of the warpstorm, the waves rose to half that height, battering the cliffs with such force the spray drenched the land above. The wind howled with voices. It raged against the Space Wolves as they cornered the daemonic hordes. The abominations of the Ruinous Powers shrieked and gibbered, their voices entwining with the wind and waves.

They fought in vain. The true tempest came from Fenris.

Harald turned his doubts into rage as he and his brothers crashed into the final hordes. On all sides, the Deathwolves howled with triumph. After weeks of incessant battle, they attacked as if fresh to the battlefield. Their prey had nowhere to turn. They tore into the daemons with furious joy. Ichor and spray drenched Harald as he and Icetooth savaged them, and Glacius seemed to sing in his hand. He barely felt the impact of his blows. He cut through skulls and chopped torsos in half. He crushed spines with his storm shield. He fired into explosions of disintegrating wyrdflesh.

Canis laughed with merciless ferocity. Harald joined him. So did the entire cavalry, and then the infantry. The cliffs resounded with the terrible laughter of alpha predators.

Harald and Icetooth plunged forwards, and forwards again, until there was no forwards any longer.

The shattered daemon army plunged over the edge of the cliffs. Monstrous forms struggled through the air. Waves like mountains rose to swallow them, Nurades in its anger taking its tormentors into the violent depths of the sea.

The Deathwolves' laughter rode the thunder of the surf.

Lord Governor Elsener met with Harald Deathwolf and Canis Wolfborn in one of the defence spires of Hive Genos. Elsener's quarters had been destroyed early in the incursion. He had barely escaped the tower's fall. None of the astropaths lower down had been as fortunate. Their cry for help had been their last act, and it had opened them fatally to the power of the warp. Elsener had witnessed their daemonic transformation. He had witnessed much since the start of the war. He had seen thousands of hive militia and all but a handful of his Tempestus honour guard give their lives in the defence of a chapel redoubt in the centre of the hive. He caught sight of his reflection in a glassteel window as he approached the chamber. What he had seen was branded on his face. His eyes were sunken and his skin was grey and lined with the deep scars of a soul's trauma. He saw the face of a man who would not live long past the end of the war.

The Emperor grant I see the liberation of Nurades, he thought.

He entered the room, leaning on a rough cane he had fashioned from the shaft of an ornamental pike. The chamber was a turret emplacement midway up the tower. It was large enough to serve as a command centre, and it was intact. Heavy bolters stood in the vaulted apertures facing north, south, east and west. They guarded the approaches over the rooftops of the lower hab complexes. Or the ruins of those complexes. Much of Genos was a smouldering ruin. But it had been cleansed.

The sky was dark with the smoke from the fires. It was free of the lunatic brilliance of the warp storm. As the war swept upwards from the Lacertus Peninsula on the inhabited northern land mass of Nurades, the strength of the storm faded. It had been many days now since Genos and Predomitus had been free of the terrors of that light and its rains.

Waiting for the lord governor was the liberation of Nurades. Elsener's breath caught. Two colossal warriors faced him. Their armour carried the stench of war. There was the acrid sting of fyceline, and the disturbing trace of slaughtered abominations in the streaks of ichor. And the aura of dangerous animals. They were human, yet their features were so rough-hewn, their hair so wild, that Elsener felt he had stepped into the presence of massive beasts.

He feared them almost as much as the things he had been fighting for weeks.

Elsener bowed, eyes averted. 'My lords,' he said. 'Nurades thanks you for the salvation you bring.'

Deathwolf grunted. 'Your survival does you credit, Lord Elsener.' He turned to the hololith table that had been brought to the chamber. 'We have some questions for you.' The table displayed a map of Nurades' polar regions. 'The war grows fiercer the further north we go,' Deathwolf said.

With an effort, Elsener forced himself not to imagine a plague of horrors even worse than that which had attacked Genos.

'The abominations are more numerous, and more resolved to prevent our advance,' Deathwolf continued. He tapped the map where runes indicated some form of complex. 'What is this? I have found no records about it.'

'Borassus,' Elsener said. He swallowed and leaned more heavily on his cane. 'We expunged the records, but we have yet to erase its memory from our culture. It is a fortification. It is cursed.'

Wolfborn snorted. 'What on Nurades is not?'

'Borassus has been a place of shadows for centuries. It has been shunned since long before the warp storm came.'

'So it will be all the worse now, you believe,' Deathwolf said.

'How can it not be?'

Deathwolf nodded. 'We take note of your warning. No son of Fenris takes the word *curse* lightly. So Borassus is where we must go. If the Ruinous Powers seek to prevent us from reaching it, its importance is clear.' He spread his hand over the polar regions. 'There are no settlements for over a thousand kilometres in any direction. No prey for the daemons. Borassus is their anchor point on this continent. From what you say, it may also be a gateway for them. We shall take it, and cleanse this world.'

The skies were clear over Borassus as the Stormwolves arrived. There was no smog of heavy industry in this empty region, a land of barren rock and deep cold. Nor were there the unholy flames of the warp storm. Even as the Deathwolves had prepared their assault on the fortifications, the convulsion around Nurades had subsided. The storm had passed. The materium was reasserting itself. The night of the Nurades' pole was a clean black and the stars were jagged silver. Twice the size of Luna, Nurades' moon cast a light heavy with silence over Borassus.

A hundred kilometres to the south, the heavy armour of the Deathwolves battled a massive surge of daemons in the mountain pass that was the primary access point to the Borassus region across land. With the attention of the forces of Chaos drawn to that struggle, Harald ordered an air insertion into the target zone. Now the Space Wolves came in waves of gunships, disembarking on a wide plain before the main gate of the fortifications.

As his cavalry and infantry assembled, Harald eyed the battlements, outlined in black by the vast sphere of the moon. The complex of bunkers, towers and ramparts made him think of broken tusks and fangs. Borassus hulked, quiet and black, waiting. The main gate was a ruin. The way in was clear. He saw no movement.

Standing beside him, Canis said, 'This place is not dead.' His fangs were bared. Icetooth and Fangir growled. Their hackles were raised.

'It waits for us,' Harald agreed.

The cavalry of the Deathwolves advanced with caution. Harald could not lead a charge with no enemy in sight.

The Space Wolves passed through the ruined gate. Beyond was a large staging ground. Some of the barracks surrounding it had fallen in on themselves. Rockcrete walls had tumbled as if smashed by a huge fist. Bunkers were squat shapes, at regular intervals in the space between the walls and the great hulk of the central keep. Cold light and deep shadow washed over them. Their doorways and turret apertures gaped, idiot mouths and blind glares. Harald sent squads ahead to check the nearest buildings. They found only darkness inside.

The Deathwolves moved deeper into Borassus. Wind whispered over the ground, cold with loss. The tread of thunderwolf paws and ceramite boots echoed against the walls, and desolation embraced the company.

The door to the keep had fallen too. Harald slowed when he saw the entrance was blocked with rubble. The interior of the keep appeared to have collapsed. He scanned the upper levels of squat towers. Rows of apertures stared back at him; more dark, empty eyes.

The eyes blinked and snarling light burst from them. It lit the ramparts of the keep. On the roofs of the bunkers, as if a concealing curtain had been ripped away, flame daemons of Tzeentch now whirled their mad dance and hurled daemonic fire at the company. *They've been there all along*, Harald realised. Some great sorcery had kept them hidden.

The blasts hit everywhere across the Deathwolves' formation. A fireball of coruscating blue streaked past Harald's shoulder. It hit Aluar, enveloping the Grey Hunter. Power armour, flesh, bone and muscle mutated and fused with such explosive energy that he passed from a thing of bleeding angles and howling mouths to ash in a fraction of a second.

On all sides, reality cracked. An army appeared in mid-charge, tearing through the brittle veil of the real. The staging ground was empty and then it was full. A stampede of juggernauts barrelled into the Deathwolves' flanks. They were massive beasts of crimson hide and crimson armour with horns that were as long as their jaws. Some horns were spikes, while some were in the shape of serrated axe blades, and behind each was the force of a speeding tank. They pierced ceramite. They chopped through ribs. They impaled thunderwolves through the throat.

Riding high on their monstrous steeds, Khornate swordlings swung their blades down onto damaged armour. They exulted with each skull they severed, holding high their crimson offerings to Khorne.

Slower and more numerous than the behemoth cavalry, thousands of daemons of Nurgle closed in. They were a sea of droning, chanting pestilence. Weeping sores covered their bodies and maggots dropped, squirming, from their blades. They came to smother the Deathwolves in the embrace of the grandfather of disease.

'Form up!' Harald voxed. 'Push them back!' Icetooth and Fangir lunged towards the stampeding Khornate daemons.

'Cowards, depending on surprise,' Canis snarled.

It worked, Harald thought. 'Then we'll render their tactic futile,' he vowed. The trap had been sprung. He would take the Deathwolves out of it now. The beast in his heart swore this, though the cold tactician reckoned the odds and knew how this night would end.

The scarlet behemoths attacked the Space Wolves flanks. There was no way forward. The ruined keep was a cliff wall. The only chance was to break the brunt of the assault and reclaim mobility.

'We must push to the rear,' Harald said to Canis. He poured bolt shells into the skull of a leviathan until its head burst. It fell heavily, carving a furrow in the stony ground, rolling over and crushing its rider.

'A retreat?' Canis asked. Fangir dodged a charge and dug his claws into the monster's scales. Canis decapitated the swordling with a swipe of his right hand and impaled the behemoth's neck with the wolf claws on his left.

'A manoeuvre,' Harald said. 'With a change of prey.'

'Brothers!' he shouted into the vox. 'Rend the daemons of plague apart!' He began to turn Icetooth around. A juggernaut launched itself at the thunderwolf. Icetooth twisted around, brought his head down and latched his jaws onto the beast's throat. He bit with steel-crunching force. Daemonic ichor poured to the ground as the juggernaut bellowed and tried to shake free. Harald batted aside the sword daemon's weapon with his bolt pistol and slammed Glacius into the abomination's midsection, cutting it in half. It dissolved into steaming, scarlet foulness. Icetooth tightened his grip on the juggernaut. His claws smashed through its armour. Harald turned his axe at the exposed flesh, hacking deep into the body of the monster. It reared backwards with a strength born of its impending doom. Icetooth rose on his hindquarters with it. The juggernaut tried to roll over and crush its tormentors, but it was evenly matched with the thunderwolf. As if he was as furious with the ambush as his master, Icetooth refused to release his prey. The juggernaut fell back on all fours and Icetooth tore its throat out. It slumped down, and Harald cut off its head.

The huge daemon's body collapsed in on itself. Its scales rusted, then flaked to dust, and its flesh melted into a foul muck. As its mass disappeared, Harald had the room to manoeuvre. Beside him, Canis and Fangir finished the other behemoth. Fangir clawed all the way through the flank, loosing a flood of snapping, shrieking, burning viscera. Canis cut deeper with his own blades until he severed the skull. The daemon's roar of pain and rage choked off and the monster vanished in an explosion of ichor. Moving to the left and right flanks, Wolf Lord and champion barrelled down the line of the Deathwolves, adding their might to that of each brother locked in a struggle, blunting the assault of the daemon cavalry.

'Back to the walls! Back to the plain!' Harald ordered. 'There we will run the abominations down!'

The Great Company changed its direction. The Deathwolves fought through the jaws and crush of the Khornate monsters. They fought through the barrage of warp flame that fell in their midst, destroying their brothers through lethal metamorphosis. And they moved against the plaguebearers.

Overhead, the Stormwolves strafed the ramparts with helfrost and las. Stormfang gunships punished the daemons on the ground. Great beams created swaths of absolute zero temperatures. Some of the daemons caught in the fire managed to move, their unnatural being performing the impossible, yet they crumbled apart as they advanced, reduced to dust before they could be free.

The Tzeetchian flame daemons retaliated in force. Across the fortifications, half of them redirected their fire at the gunships and assault craft. Warpfire engulfed engines. It turned wings into fangs. Before Harald could reach the rear lines, multiple volleys of the unholy flame gripped the fuselage of a Stormfang, transforming it into something scaled and flexible. Engines screamed and the gunship whirled. Its sudden flesh changed again. It became glass. The forces of its violent movement shattered it. Ship and crew vanished in an explosion that lit the dark with light natural and unnatural.

Harald and Canis rejoined each other as the Deathwolves struck hard against the plague daemons. The abominations at the front disappeared in mid chant, annihilated by the massed rage of the Space Wolves. The cold polar air became dank and humid with rot. Even as they disintegrated, the daemons fought back, releasing a wall of noxious vapour ahead of them.

The Deathwolves advanced into the sea of disease. Though the behemoths continued their attack, they had lost the advantage of speed. They were bogged down as they waded through the plague daemons. The Great Company drew closer to the gate, and the freedom of movement beyond.

Warpflame surrounded the Stormwolf *Guard of Frostheim*. A score of flame daemons hit it at the same time. Its frame subjected itself to conflicting forces of such power it froze in mid-flight. Madness held it suspended over the gateway. It bulged and contracted. It writhed. Eyes tore open and bled along the fuselage. The underbelly split wide. Its teeth gnashed, and then it screamed.

'*Back!*' Harald roared.

The company's movement stalled. A mass so great could not reverse course that suddenly. The Space Wolves reacted with perfect discipline, yet for fateful seconds they neither advanced nor retreated.

Guard of Frostheim fell. A combusting assemblage of metal and flesh crashed into the ground before the gate. The incinerating blast washed over the Deathwolves. There could be no turning for Harald, and he leaned into the explosion, fastening his grip on his mantle as Icetooth crouched low, howling at the destruction. The cowling of an engine cartwheeled over Harald's head. It came down in the Grey Hunters behind him, both blade and meteor. A wind of ignited plasma and burning immaterium raged around him. It sought to devour him. It failed, repelled by his cloak. Made from the hide of the ice troll king he had slain, it defied all flame.

The sound of the explosion was so huge that it drowned out the cries of the dying, yet Harald knew his brothers were being consumed. He could feel the loss in his soul. In grief and rage, he rose before the gale of *Guard of Frostheim*'s death had fully abated. Icetooth's hide smouldered. Patches of fur and flesh had been burned down to muscle. Matching his rider's fury, he answered Harald's command and lunged upward.

'With me, brothers!' Harald voxed. 'Gather and face the foe together. Let the abominations break against the rock of our strength! Cavalry, prepare to rush the enemy towards the keep! Infantry, break with us and scale the walls.'

The gate was rubble. There was no egress from Borassus. Scores of daemons had vanished in the crash, for all the difference that made. The tide of plaguebearers still ran high.

The beast in Harald could not silence the tactician. The breakout attempt had failed. The last chance to escape the trap had fallen with *Guard of Frostheim*. One last charge, then. One last bellow of rage against the enemy. If the cavalry drew the greater part of the daemons away from his brothers on foot, perhaps the Deathwolf infantry would survive to rejoin the heavy armour to the south. If the saga of the company's thunderwolves ended here, let it be a fitting conclusion, a song echoing with the death of countless unholy foes.

Sensing vulnerability, the daemon horde redoubled its attack. The roaring beasts shook the ground in their raging hunger. A clamour of tolling bells urged the plague daemons on. Blades of disease and blades of wrath hacked at the Space Wolves. Harald's warriors gathered around him forming a wall of snarling beasts and ceramite-clad giants. The constant barrage of warpflame struck more down with every second. The daemons of Khorne and Nurgle pressed in, the closing of a vice.

Canis Wolfborn had come through the explosion with his face a single massive burn. His armour was scorched black. His eyes shone with proud anger. 'Predators to the last,' he said to Harald.

Harald nodded. Canis was ready for the inevitable, eager for the kills he would yet be granted this night. This was good, it was right. Harald raised Glacius in his last defiance.

'For Russ!' he called.

'For the Wolftime!' the company answered.

For us, it has come, Harald thought.

He felt the hair on his arms rise. He was surrounded by foulness that would drive mortals insane, but something else in the night made him react as if to an unknown threat.

A flicker rippled over the daemons. It looked like uncertainty.

Shadows streaked across the rooftops before huge silhouettes struck the flame daemons and tore them apart. The warpfire barrage came to a sudden end. In its wake came a deluge from the air. It was ichor. So many daemons were destroyed in a matter of seconds that their end was a rain upon the battlefield. Harald blinked. The shapes were monstrous, but not as strange as they should be. He heard growls, deep and ferocious, and his blood stirred with recognition.

His olfactory senses responded to the scent of kinship.

'Brothers...' Canis said with stunned awe.

'How?' said Harald. This isn't possible, he thought. The shapes were too big. Too misshapen.

And yet...

He would wonder later. On every roof of Borassus, the daemons were being exterminated.

Harald signalled the charge, and already it was no longer desperate. The Deathwolves howled their challenge as they attacked.

The figures on the roofs howled back.

No, Harald thought again. He cracked the skull of a behemoth wide open, stitched a swordling from head to belly with bolt shells, and again he thought *no*, torn by hope and unease before the impossible.

Now the ramparts of Borassus were free of daemons. The figures that could not be familiar leapt to the ground. They attacked the rear ranks of the daemons, butchering their way towards the Deathwolves. They used no firearms. Some had punch-daggers. They attacked with the pure savagery of the animal, shredding the enemy with their hands. Their clawed hands.

A greater monstrosity overwhelmed the daemons. The Deathwolves fought with the boiling rage of near defeat. Their every howl was answered by the giants approaching them. Now the momentum was with the thunderwolves. Now it was the daemons who were surrounded.

Now it was the daemons who were doomed.

The end was inevitable. It came quickly. And when the last daemonic remains were dissolving in their foulness, Harald faced the creatures who could not be there.

The heavy moonlight reigned over Borassus again. Its quiet was broken by the predatory breathing of giants.

The monsters were hunched as if ready to spring. They did not. They held back – for the moment.

Canis was growling in unison with the thunderwolves.

Harald looked at him. 'You called them brothers,' he said.

Canis nodded, shook his head. He grimaced in confusion. 'They are, but... their scent is strange. It is *old*.' His fists opened and closed. He was caught between the signals of kin and threat. He was on the threshold of attacking.

'Hold fast, brother,' Harald said. His weapons held low but at the ready, he advanced towards the creatures who had saved his warriors. With every detail he took in, the vertigo of unreality grew stronger. They were huge. Very tall and massively broad, they dwarfed Harald. They were beasts.

They were wolves.

They hunched forwards as if running on all fours came naturally to them, and indeed their arms were long. Their faces too were elongated and hirsute. Their fangs were huge, and their maws so lupine Harald wondered if they could speak. There were still aspects of the human in the monsters though; he saw in those faces the thing he had tried to deny but could no longer. He saw the familiar. He saw *kinship*. He smelled it too, beneath the tang of combat stimulants and thick bestial musk.

The wolves wore armour. How did the firmament not crack wide open to see such armour in this place and in this time? It was battered, patchwork, barely held together by rough welds, damaged almost beyond recognition. Almost. It was a faded slate grey, the colour of ancient history. The insignia were visible, though close to vanishing beneath battle scars. They were Fenrisian. They were known to Harald. They were known to every Space Wolf. Their memory had been faithfully preserved.

They had not been seen for ten thousand years.

'This cannot be!' a Wolf Guard shouted. For a moment, Harald thought the words were in his head.

No, he thought. This cannot be.

The 13th Great Company. Lost to the warp in pursuit of Magnus after the fall of Prospero.

The immense warriors grouped around the largest of them all. The night rumbled with low, wary growls. Harald maglocked his weapons. He held his hands open and away from his sides. He approached the alpha. The great beast watched him with amber eyes. He was so huge that his mooncast shadow swallowed the Deathwolf.

Harald held the gaze of those eyes, even as he had to crane his head back. I do not come to attack, he thought, but I do come to command. He knew this was necessary. Yet he was closing in on a myth. It was an effort to keep the awe he felt from his face.

He was only a few steps away now. He saw the beast's features in more detail. The traces of the human were clearer. The shape of the eyes, of the brows – more and more he saw the lineaments he knew in his brothers, and in his own reflection.

He accepted the truth of what he saw. The murmurs and warning growls of the Deathwolves behind him were an assurance he was not hallucinating.

Harald stopped before the alpha. He stood straight, his gaze unwavering. The great beast's chest expanded as it took a breath. The alpha rumbled.

Harald braced.

The beast lowered his head and dropped to one knee. So did all the others. The threat of the moment passed as they acknowledged a new alpha.

Though he dreaded what these revenants portended, Harald was mindful of the debt he owed them too. He placed his hand on the giant's shoulder and bid him rise.

'Who are you?' he asked.

The monster's jaw struggled to shape a name. 'Yngvir,' he said.

'Are you loyal to the primarch?' Harald asked.

'We... are... brother.' The rasp was entirely animal. Only the words were human. 'We... are... Wulfen.'

Why Nurades? Harald thought again. Now you know. He looked at the ranks of the Wulfen, and felt he was gazing into a future seized and made bloody by the jaws of the past.

CHAPTER 2

The Council of Wolves

Dark Angels Company Master Araphil came to Borassus to hunt for truth. A war had come and gone, and it had left behind shadows. Summoned by Scouts, his company had pierced the warp storm and entered orbit over the polar circle of Nurades. At that moment, the world had still been overrun with daemons. By the time the landing was complete, the daemons were gone. How?

The marks of battle were everywhere amid the ruined fortifications. The struggle here had been ferocious. The buildings and the ground were scorched and blasted. The walls were pocked with the distinctive impact craters of bolter shells. Other Space Marines had been here. Who?

Until a few moments ago, the most urgent question had been where Sergeant Arhad and his Scouts had gone. They had vanished from all vox and auspex readings before Araphil's company had arrived at Nurades. Now Araphil had partial answers, although dark ones. The shadows were deep, but he would hunt out what they concealed.

He stood in a bunker, surrounded by the remains of the Scouts. The bunker had become an abattoir. The bodies were dismembered, heads torn in half. Viscera had been thrown against the walls and hung over the ledges of gun apertures. Even in the cold of this region of Nurades, the atmosphere of the chamber was clammy with the stench of blood. The Scouts' armour had long, parallel rents. The sign of claws.

Who has done this? That was the urgent question. The obvious answer was *daemons*. Araphil mistrusted it. For all the savagery, for all the butchery, the kills were too clean. Where were the signature desecrations of the Ruinous Powers? It was conceivable that the sheer brutality was a form of Khornate rage. Araphil was unsatisfied with that answer too. He sniffed. His neuroglottis detected the faint trace of animal musk beneath the overwhelming odours of vitae and of bodies turned inside out. Araphil could believe animals had been at work here but he could think of none native to Nurades capable of overcoming even a single Scout.

Outside the bunker, squads moved through the wreckage of Borassus, seeking truth and secrets. After he had been called here, he had commanded the scene be left to him alone. He wished to commune with the space and the dead on his own. He moved deeper into the bunker, taking in each corpse, recording each name with a prayer and a promise of vengeance, eyeing the wounds and the manner of death. He kept his emotions in check.

Observe. Judge later. Observe now. Let the shadows speak. Let the dead give their answers.

To his right, there was a mound of body parts. Were there three victims there, or five? Perhaps portions of more. Something inside the mound moved. The motion was slight, a weak spasm. It was enough to dislodge a hand. Araphil knelt. He cleared away the fragments of corpse until he found the whole body beneath. It was Brother Dolutas. He was difficult to recognise: his face had been clawed to the bone. His armour was peeled back over his ravaged chest and broken ribs. Araphil looked closely, and Dolutas took a breath. It was weak, shallow. It could have been a sigh before dying. Then it came again.

'You have been strong, brother,' Araphil said softly. 'Apothecary!' he voxed. To the Scout he said, 'Be content. We are here to give you strength now.'

A blinking light midway down Dolutas' right flank drew Araphil's gaze. A servo-skull lay there. Its lower half was smashed and its gravitic impellers were wrecked, but one eye blinked red, red, red. The memory light. The servo-skull had preserved a recording.

Red, red, red, the eye blinked.

Answers, answers, answers.

'There are other wyrdstorms,' Logan Grimnar announced. 'Storms with the same empiric signatures as the one over Nurades. The astropaths are emphatic. Some died as they confirmed the nature of the storms, and their flesh was marked by the same wyrdflame burns in each case. The storms are scattered, yet they are unmistakable.'

Silence fell over the Wolf Lords of Fenris as the implications of those words sank in. Around the periphery of the Hall of the Great Wolf, heroes of the Chapter stirred. Serfs froze, sensing a rise in tension. It was, Harald thought, as if a great wind were gusting through the Hall. The totems and pelts on the walls did not stir, but the thunderwolves crouched at their masters' feet raised their hackles. A raven took to the air above Ulrik the Slayer. Its caw echoed across the hall.

In the centre of the vast space was the Grand Annulus. Set into the floor were thirteen wedge-shaped stone slabs, each marked with the runes and insignia of a Great Company. The Wolf Lords stood upon the territorial markers of their authority. One of the slabs was obsidian. It bore no markings. It was the painful absence on the Annulus, the break in the circle. It was the place belonging to the lost 13th Company, and so it represented all the lost. Only now the lost had been found. Harald's gaze kept returning to it. So did the eyes of the other Wolf Lords.

Krom Dragongaze broke the silence, speaking the question on every mind. 'What do the storms portend?' he asked.

Grimnar turned to Ulrik the Slayer, standing at his side. He nodded. The Wolf Priest advanced to the centre of the Annulus.

'I have spoken with Yngvir,' he said with a voice ancient yet strong like grating stone. 'Though his speech is difficult, he was clear that there are more of his brothers coming. *On the wings of storm.* Those are his words.'

'And this return,' Dragongaze said before anyone else could respond, 'if these Wulfen are indeed the Thirteenth, why now? How has it happened? What does it mean?'

The Slayer waited several beats before answering. Now the silence in the Hall was total. 'The omen of the Wulfen is clear,' he said. 'If they have come back, can Russ be far behind?'

The Hall of the Great Wolf erupted.

'How can we be sure?' Gunnar Red Moon demanded. 'Where is the proof? How do we even know the Wulfen are what they claim to be?'

'Their existence speaks for them,' Sven Bloodhowl answered. 'As do their deeds. They saved Lord Deathwolf.' He looked at Harald. 'You who are brother to more wolves in your company than any of us must feel the truth of our kinship with the Thirteenth.'

Harold gave Bloodhowl a long look. The other Wolf Lord was much younger than he was. His hair and beard were a rich brown, and cut short. His symmetrical, rock-jawed features were indeed much further from the lupine than Harald's. He would feel the complexities and risks of the warrior's relationship with the beasts less acutely.

'We are kin to wolves,' Harald said. 'We are *as* wolves. We are not wolves. You can see what they have become.'

He kept his tone moderate, but his words enflamed tempers even more. The Wolf Lords moved towards the centre of the Annulus as they shouted at each other. Harald held back. He had expressed his doubts, said what he had to say. The monstrosity of the Wulfen gave him pause, and there were too many unanswered questions about what had happened on Nurades. He could not easily accept the Slayer's pronouncement, though he could not dismiss it either.

The other Wolf Lords were far more vehement.

'Lord Deathwolf is right!' Kjarl Grimblood said. 'Look what they have become! An omen indeed! A dark one!'

'How do we know they are really Wulfenkind?' said Egil Iron Wolf. 'Why not mutations? After so long in the warp, their Canis Helix could have suffered terrible damage.'

Erik Morkai snorted. 'Monsters or not, what does it matter? They fight well. They're good weapons.'

'Nothing more?' Bran Redmaw rounded on Morkai. 'Is that the depth of your thought and honour? And my war packs, are we the same to you? Savages to be used up as needed?'

'You hot-blooded fool, did I say that?'

'You as good as did,' Redmaw told Morkai. 'If that is all you can see in the Wulfen, you are more blind than I ever imagined!'

The voices rose in anger. Harald looked to the Slayer. The Wolf Priest was regarding him silently. Harald thought of the meeting in the vaults. That was the first omen. How did the Slayer interpret that night? How did he believe it linked to the return of the Wulfen? Harald was convinced the link was there. He could not divine its meaning, nor could he shake his unease.

'The Fell-Handed!' Krom was saying. He said it again, cutting through the shouts. 'We must consult Bjorn the Fell-Handed. He *knew* the Thirteenth. He was there before the company vanished.'

All eyes turned to Ulrik the Slayer. He shook his head. 'Bjorn will not awaken,' he said.

'Good omen or ill,' said Ragnar Blackmane, 'we must find the others.'

No one disagreed.

Grimnar strode forward. The Wolf Lords stood still. They waited for the Great Wolf to speak.

'Our task is clear,' he said. 'We will seek out and return our brothers to Fenris. Whether they are cursed, or whether their arrival means Russ will soon be at our side again,' he nodded once to Ulrik, 'we will know in the end. And know we must.'

Harald nodded at this.

'Brothers, make ready. We sail the Sea of Stars with the Wulfen to gather the Thirteenth Great Company!'

As the Wolf Lords left the Hall, Dragongaze drew Harald aside. 'You're worried,' he said.

'I believe the Slayer and I see very different omens in the Wulfen. He sees what we lost, and what we hope to have again.'

'And what do you see?'

'What we might become if we are not vigilant. I see what we might lose.'

'You think the Wulfen are harbingers of disaster?'

'I'm sure they are harbingers. I don't know of what. That is my concern.'

'Our meeting before the Murderfang...' Dragongaze began.

'Yes,' said Harald. 'I was thinking of that too. It is linked to Nurades. But how? What drew us there. Krom, a daemon laughed at us as we vanquished it.'

Dragongaze was silent for a moment. 'Yet you purged the daemons,' he said. 'You defeated the Ruinous Powers.'

'Even so, the daemon laughed.'

'Daemonic malice?' Dragongaze suggested. 'It sought to sow doubt.'

'Yes,' said Harald. He met Dragongaze's eyes squarely, and did not hide the depths of his concern. 'It succeeded.'

At war in the world beneath sleep, above death. The struggle eternal. Ten thousand years now, fighting from plane to plane, an unending march.

I tarry until you come again, father.

The loss of the body is no loss of self. The agility of youth forgotten in the great hulk that fights in the kingdom above sleep. But here, in the land between, there is speed again. The fury of spirit matched to the echo of form. The echo of a sarcophagus, a coffin of false death and infinite war.

All echoes here. Shadows of form and thought, cast by the weight of things in the other realm, the one above sleep. The roots run deep. The war runs deeper. So long without surcease, but what need for rest here, in the kingdom beneath?

None.

Only battle.

On the echo ramparts of the echo fortress, fighting an enemy who are not echoes, whose flesh is the stuff of echoes.

I must wake. I must speak to my brothers.

A flood of daemons, a sea lapping at the hexagrammic shadow. There can be no waking yet. The sea is rising.

The daemons must be fought.

The prey tried to fight back. Lasgun fire struck the Wulfen. The beasts ran directly into the fire, roaring. They were twice the size of the puny human figures, and much faster. They ripped arms from torsos and heads from necks. Blood fountained across the scene of the massacre and paving stones shook under one monster's feet as he rushed an opponent. He wielded an immense frost axe. He sliced the body in half with a stroke so powerful the blade buried itself in the wall behind then freed it and held it aloft with both hands. The slaughter was complete. The Wulfen pack howled as one.

They looked up to the gallery where Logan Grimnar stood with the Iron Priest Hrothgar Swordfang. The Wulfen panted, their breath steaming, blood coating their muzzles and armour. They were surrounded by the torn flesh and scattered viscera of the training servitors. They were the image of mindless savagery.

The beasts lowered their heads and took a knee, bowing to the supreme alpha.

'Good,' Grimnar said.

That was enough. The Wulfen rose and loped from the training arena.

'Their new armour looks well,' Grimnar said to Swordfang.

'Thank you, Great Wolf,' the Iron Priest said. 'Their Mark II relics were beyond repair. We completed the Mark VIII size modifications four days ago. They were reluctant to part with their remnants, but they have adapted.'

'Has communication improved?'

Swordfang's servo-arms moved back and forth equivocally. 'A little,' he said. 'Serkir, the one with the frost axe, is interesting. He is volatile. He can be almost articulate in short bursts. At other times, language escapes him completely. He understands more than most of the others, I think.'

'A leader?'

'He is subordinate to Yngvir. He might do well with his own pack, though.'

Treaded servitors entered the arena from low access doors. Their arms had been replaced with floor-scraping blades. Blank-eyed, unemotional, they began the disposal of the bloody remains.

'The weapons the Wulfen were using,' Grimnar said. 'I saw no firearms.'

'No,' said Swordfang. 'They appear to have no aptitude or taste for them.'

'Those swords and axes, they look familiar. But I don't recognise them from our arsenals.' They were too huge. They were impractical for any warrior who wasn't as outsized as the Wulfen.

'They are from our walls, Great Wolf.'

Grimnar blinked, surprised, as he realised what Swordfang meant. Immense relic weapons had hung on the walls of the Fang for millennia. Grimnar had regarded them as he did the heroic tapestries. They were heraldry, ornamentation, ancient objects to be honoured.

'What inspired you to take them down?' he asked.

'Serkir seized the axe himself as we crossed a hall to the training grounds,' Swordfang said. 'He cut a statue in half with it. He seemed familiar with its balance. So did the other Wulfen when I ordered the gathering of other such weapons. They wield the weapons as if the blades were forged for this express purpose.'

'What are you suggesting? That they were already in their current form ten thousand years ago?'

'I do not think so. The remnants of the power armour they wore show signs of stress, suggesting they burst through it when they changed.'

Grimnar frowned. 'I do not understand.'

'Nor do I. Then there are the grenades. I instigated a full search for all relics scaled to the proportions of the Wulfen. We found many swords and axes. Enough for the entire company, should all the brothers be found. The grenades, however, are not just suited to the hands of the Wulfen. They are suited to their brains.'

'What do you mean?'

'I was not sure the Wulfen would be capable of using explosives. Firearms are too complex. Nevertheless, we included the grenades in the trials. We discovered they are not on timers.'

'Impact fuses?'

'No. An impulse trigger.'

'Those are very rare,' Grimnar said.

'These are rarer still. I attempted to operate one. I cannot. But the Wulfen can do so without difficulty. The triggers associated with these grenades are attuned to the specific neural patterns of the Wulfen.'

Grimnar digested this in silence for a long moment. 'What do you conclude?' he asked Swordfang.

'I cannot conclude anything,' Hrothgar answered. 'We are faced with two possibilities. Either the phenomenon of the Wulfen existed in our deep past, though there are no records or tales of their existence, in or out of the Thirteenth Company...'

'Or?'

'Or these weapons were forged in *anticipation* of the coming of the Wulfen.'

The thought stole Grimnar's breath. Had this moment been building for ten thousand years? 'They were foretold?' he asked.

'I know of no such prophecy.'

'Nor do I.' That did not mean none existed. So much had been forgotten over a hundred centuries. If in some way the Wulfen were not just returned but long awaited, then Ulrik the Slayer's interpretation of the omens must be correct.

Grimnar did not want to contemplate the implications if the Wolf Priest were wrong.

The launch bays of the Fang vibrated with the roar of gunship engines. Squad after squad embarked in the assault craft. The bays were open and the wind of Fenris shrieked inside, freezing the skin, biting deep, stirring the blood to the hunt and to war. The sky beyond was streaked by the contrails of the gunships that had already left, ascending to the strike cruisers waiting at low anchor. One Great Company after another departed Fenris to set sail on this most portentous of hunts.

All but the Tenth. The Drakeslayers would remain.

Krom Dragongaze stood on an observation platform above the bay, unblinking in the backwash of motors and the merciless fangs of the wind. He stared into the bay. He did not turn his head until, in the corner of his eye, he saw Grimnar approach. Then he faced the Great Wolf.

'The Fang is yours,' Grimnar said.

'While all the other Wolf Lords depart on this most vital of missions.'

'Fenris cannot be left undefended.'

Krom lowered his head in acknowledgement. There is no need for a Wolf Lord to remain as castellan, he thought. Or for an entire company to be sidelined.

As if reading his mind, Grimnar said, 'I gave this task to you and the Tenth for a reason.'

Krom waited, saying nothing.

'You were reckless on Alaric Prime,' Grimnar said.

So this is punishment for the Sanctus Reach, Krom thought.

'I need to know you will keep faith in your oaths,' said Grimnar.

Krom bristled. He struggled to remain silent. He succeeded. Just. Grimnar continued, 'There is no question of loyalty or ability. The issue is discipline.'

The urge to protest was strong. Krom's frustration was motivated by more than slighted honour. The meeting at the Murderfang's vault haunted him; the portents were multiplying. Though the Slayer's talk of Russ' return was compelling, it did not satisfy Krom. Harald's part in the unfolding saga was already fateful. Krom had no doubt that more was to come. He and the Slayer had yet to learn their roles. The Wolf Priest would find the thread of his destiny in the Sea of Stars while Krom would remain here and wait. There was something he must do. There was a reason he had been among the three to be led to that encounter. It must have something to do with the Wulfen. How could he do what fate required of him, whatever that was, if he was cantoned on Fenris?

No matter. There was no choice. The Great Wolf had spoken and Krom's path was clear. He quashed his protestations and nodded once, his face immobile as stone.

'I make my oath that Fenris will be secure,' he said. 'The Drakeslayers stand fast.' He was called to this task, and he would fulfil it. Glory was as nothing compared to an oath and redemption.

'I am pleased to hear it,' said Grimnar. 'A pack of the Wulfen will remain with you. Iron Priest Swordfang will continue his examination of them. There are many questions that need to be answered. We will not learn all of them on the Sea of Stars.'

Krom nodded once more. He wondered how he should interpret the news that not all the Wulfen would depart. He watched Grimnar walk away. A minute later the Great Wolf appeared in the bay below, surrounded by Ulrik the Slayer, the High Rune Priest Njal Stormcaller, and the champion Arjac Rockfist. The legends marched up the assault ramp into the Thunderhawk that would transport them to the battle-barge *Allfather's Honour*. The roar of the transport's engines built to deafening levels, then it shot out of the launch bay.

The fiery wind of its departure was the last one. Krom remained as he was, watching the final Stormwolves climb while the bay doors rumbled together, shutting out the gale of Fenris. Premonition crawled over his flesh. His hackles rose. When the doors clanged, the ring of iron against iron was the doleful slam of a sarcophagus lid.

He knew then that fate would still find him.

PART 2: THE HUNT

CHAPTER 3

Whitestalker

The mechanism had not moved in centuries. It was inert, an assemblage of cold shadow and utter immobility. Nonetheless, its daily care was observed as a duty sacred and vital. Armatures and spheres of brass and silver and gold gleamed in sepulchral perfection. Its gears were anointed with holy oil. In all the millennia of its existence, there had never been a single moment when it had been left unobserved.

On this day, the Speculum Infernus moved.

A data-servant called out in alarm at the first sight of action. A single cogwheel, a few centimetres across, stirred. Within seconds, its revolutions were a blur. Larger and larger nested wheels began to turn. From the eight corners of the great device, tall sceptres crackled with eldritch lightning. Inside the periphery, spheres rotated and travelled along complex, elliptical, intersecting revolutions. Fluted bronze pipes released scalding steam, giving voice to a hissing choir.

An alchemy of movement, an omen of metal.

On the north side of the Speculum, gargoyles of gold perched on a cluster of silver pedestals. Mechanical wings unfurled and jaws opened wide in expressions of blind hunger. Data-parchment streamed from between the fangs. The servants gathered the parchment, averting their gaze from its runes and sigils. The dooms inscribed thereon were not for them to understand.

This was a mercy.

In the Citadel of Titan, the Prognosticars of the Grey Knights gathered to read the dooms. The sanctified mechanism of the Speculum Infernus shook and scribed, steamed and prophesied. It told of warp storms. It revealed connections.

The Grey Knights beheld the terrible confluence of events. They were forming a single immense shape, its meaning as unspeakable as it was inescapable.

And then, even as the Great Companies of the Space Wolves spread out across the galaxy to gather their lost kin, the Brotherhoods of the Grey Knights departed Titan on quests just as grave and urgent. The Space Wolves travelled the lines of a pattern. The Grey Knights sought to arrest its manifestation.

Elsewhere, darkness laughed.

Fimnir. Spartha IV. Dragos.

The sites of the hunt. World after world engulfed by the sudden warp storms, their empyrean signatures so distinct and so identical that they seemed to be the flowerings of a single tempest.

Hades Reach. Atrapan.

The Great Companies fell upon worlds tortured by the revels of daemons. On every planet, billions of subjects of the Imperium had no hope until feral salvation dropped out of the skies, and rioting madness gave way to war.

Suldabrax. Emberghul.

Grimnar assigned strike force names to the companies. Sagablade. Whitestalker. Iron Hunt. Kingsguard. These were not individual crusades. They were the stepping stones of a single mission on a scale rarely mounted in the history of the Chapter. The struggle on each world was enough to inspire legends in the local cultures that would last until the Wolftime. The victories were the stuff of sagas on Fenris, but they were important only in the measure of the totality of the hunt's success. The Space Wolves came to find the Wulfen. The crushing of the Ruinous Powers was a means to an end.

The surviving populations who found themselves returned to the Emperor's Light were fortunate bystanders. Had the storms that blighted their planets been of a different nature, their help would have had to come from other sources, if it came at all.

On one world after another, the Space Wolves pushed back the armies of Chaos. The splintered 13th Great Company was gathered up. The Wulfen were transported to the rallying point in the Anvarheim system. Aboard the strike cruiser *Coldfang*, under the command of Battle Leader Hjalvard, the beasts were prepared to re-enter battle, integrated into the other Companies. The 13th, for now, could not function as a unified company.

News of each success reached the other companies quickly. The Wolf Lords learned of the growing numbers of Wulfen in the ranks of their brother commanders. The victories urged Wolf Lords to greater feats.

On the *Alpha Fang*, as Strike Force Whitestalker prepared for its campaign, Harald received the reports of the hunt. He watched the tally of Wulfen warriors climb, more of them all the time, their presence growing in the martial body of the Space Wolves.

His unease grew.

'We will find every Wulfen brother before any other Imperial force,' Grimnar had declared.

'This we swear,' all the Wolf Lords had answered.

If we succeed, Harald wondered, what then?

He did not speak the question aloud. He had taken his oath.

He came close to voicing the question once. During the *Alpha Fang*'s transit through the immaterium, he asked Canis, 'What do you make of the Wulfen?'

'Strong warriors,' said the Champion.

Canis was the most feral of the Deathwolves. He was perhaps the closest of Harald's brothers to the Wulfen. Harald wanted to know if Canis felt more distance or kinship to the monsters.

'Anything more?' he asked.

'The beast is strong in them.'

'Too strong?'

Canis did not answer right away, his heavy features deep in thought. That he had to think before answering, that he seemed uncertain, was disconcerting.

'They control their frenzy,' he said at last.

'Aye, they do,' Harald said.

The conversation went no further, then. But as Harald was heading to the bridge to make ready for the drop back into the materium, Vygar Helmfang caught up to him and raised the question himself.

'Lord Deathwolf,' said the Wolf Guard, 'I understand there is no question of the Wulfen's loyalty.' *For now*, hovered unspoken in the air between them. 'But their nature...' He groped for words. 'Their form and their actions do not always coincide.' Vygar grimaced, displeased with his own formulation.

Harald understood what he meant. Any brother he had known who had even come close to resembling the Wulfen's physical form had been completely consumed by battle frenzy. He could think of no case where a Space Wolf had been capable of anything approaching calm while in that state.

They control their frenzy. Canis' comment took on greater weight.

Vygar was one of the oldest of the Wolf Guard. In the field, he fought with tenacious ferocity. He was also one of the best strategists in the company. Centuries of battle had tempered him into a warrior who understood the value of forethought. His experience and his caution were the qualities Harald prized in his strike force. And Vygar's concerns were dovetailing with Harald's own.

'You believe their nature is much more complex than some might think,' Harald said.

'I believe we know very little about it, yet are acting as if we do.'

'We are being watchful, brother. All of us.' He had faith that this was so. Even Ulrik, in his enthusiasm, was vigilant. He clapped Vygar on the shoulder plate. 'We will be vigilant together.'

Vygar nodded that he had understood. Harald was agreeing with the need for great care.

And so the *Alpha Fang* came to Svardeghul, a world of ore, an industrial cinder transformed into a malignant tumour.

The strike cruiser and its escorts translated from the immaterium into the midst of the warp storm surrounding the world. The crews of the vessels were braced. Even so, the shock struck hard. The tempest shrieked through the wounds of reality. It strained the Geller fields to breaking point. Madness found its way through fissures in the defences. It shook the hulls and laughed down corridors. Two frigates were lost. One, the Gladius-class *Roar of Asaheim*, passed before the *Alpha Fang*'s oculus. It had turned to glass. The entire vessel was a crystalline sculpture thousands of metres long. It reflected and refracted the convulsing light of the storm. Hull and weapons, decks and crew, all were translucent. The engines were silent. The vessel moved forwards with the momentum of its death.

Harald's lip curled in anger as he took in the malign beauty of the lost frigate. The doom was insidious in its art. He could not but see an ill omen in the spectacle. Then the energy of the storm took the ship. The *Roar of Asaheim* shattered, vanishing in a glistening shard cloud.

On the bridge of the *Alpha Fang*, consoles melted. A weapons-system servitor's head exploded into a mass of writhing tendrils. Feingar, pack leader of the Coldeye Scouts, stood over a hololith map with his counterpart Lokyar Longblade. The tendrils reached for Feingar, tangling around his arm. Cursing, he ripped them from his armour and crushed them to white pulp beneath his boots.

Damage reports from the fleet flooded in. Static and the sounds of claws against bone disrupted the vox transmissions.

It was several minutes before there was enough order restored on the vessel for auspex scans of Svardeghul to be possible.

'Anything?' Harald asked the mistress of the vox.

'Nothing coherent at all,' said Ager. She stood straight and to attention, but her face was grey. She alone had heard what came from the planet. She had not relayed any traffic through the vox-speakers, shielding the bridge from further madness.

She confirmed what Harald already knew from the view in the oculus. Svardeghul's only remaining ocean, remade into sludge by millennia of manufactoria effluence, was now flesh. Maws thousands of kilometres long opened and closed. This world was lost to the Imperium forever. But somewhere below, there were brothers to rescue.

Harald watched Svardeghul's agony, doubting the wisdom of his mission, but he gave the orders for it to begin.

Before the storm, Svardeghul's cities had walked. They were rigs the size of mountains. Supported by eight immense pistons, they walked the planet with seismic steps, transporting their tens of millions of workers. They moved from one ore deposit to another, sucking the planet dry of its resources and sending them off-world to feed the unending hunger of the Imperium's machinery of war. Some of the cities still walked. Augur scans revealed they had come to life. Their inhabitants had been crushed into the vitae circulating through the arteries of blind, howling monsters. Others were tottering ruins, making their slow march across the blasted land while the last of their shrieking populations were consumed by the daemons.

Wherever the augurs picked up even a semblance of conflict, Harald sent elements of Whitestalker to search for the Wulfen. He had assembled the strike force from his most experienced warriors. Even the Blood Claw band, the Deathhowls, were veterans compared to their brothers of the same rank. It would not be long before they ascended to become Grey Hunters.

'Our target is Rig Delta,' Harald told the Riders of Morkai, the Wolf Guard who would accompany him. 'It is the capital, and it has fallen silent.'

'No others have done so?' Vygar asked.

'No.' His hunting instincts were pricked by the anomaly. 'I would know why.'

'So great a fall,' said Lokyar, awed.

Harald would have marked the rare occurrence if he had not felt a chill silence in his soul. He had seen vistas of destruction beyond counting. He had seen few where vastness and suddenness were so conjoined.

The Deathwolves had made their landing before the ruins of Rig Delta, and found that it too had made a landing. Against the north end of the wreckage, a vertical precipice three thousand metres high rose above the rocky plain. Lokyar gazed back and forth from the top of the cliff to the titanic wreck. The city was so huge, even its broken corpse was almost as high as the fall it had taken.

'All the controllers of the city's march must have been killed,' Lokyar said. 'There was no one to stop it from walking over the edge.'

'Or it was made to do so,' Harald said. What daemon would not have rejoiced at causing such a catastrophe?

Portions of the great pistons still jutted skyward, driven through the base of the rig by the impact. Broken into jagged shafts, they fell away from each other, funerary columns of ruined, industrial majesty. Mining drills, refineries, manufactoria and habs were smashed into an indistinguishable mass, a hill of twisted, compacted metal. The city slumped away from the cliff, a leviathan spilling its machinic body across the plain. Promethium burned, filthy pyres lighting the contours of the rig, pooling at the bottom of the ruins into a lake. Black smoke roiled upwards towards a sky in the grip of the warp storm. Crimson and violet clouds formed into daemonic visages, their laughter tainting the air with a sick, clammy thunder.

Blood mixed with the promethium. It fell in cascades from the sharp angles of the city and flowed across the plain. Its stench was greater than the fire. The Space Wolves' nostrils were filled with the death of millions. Bodies were everywhere, burned and crushed.

They spread out for many thousands of metres on all sides of Rig Delta, a great scattering of leaves hurled to the winds when the fall came to its terrible end. There was the stink of the daemon too. Ichor dripped from collapsed frameworks. It coated the sides of machines turned into abstractions of iron and plasteel.

There was no war here, though. The event had come, and the fate of Svardeghul had moved on.

The Deathwolf drop pods had come down on the west side of Delta Rig, three quarters of the way down the length of the ruin. While the Deathwolves mustered, the Wulfen moved a short distance away and gazed off to the south. The wind blew in ever-shifting gusts, pushing the flames first one way, then the other. When it began to come from the south, the Wulfen set up a howl. They hunched further forward, as if preparing to run prey to ground. Yngvir loped back to Harald.

He stopped a respectful distance from the Wolf Lord. He lowered his head, a gesture of deference to his superior, but still Harald had to look up to meet his eyes.

'Brothers...' Ygnvir said, pointing south.

'You have their scent?' Harald said.

Ygnvir grunted. 'And daemons... War.'

'Lead us, then. We will follow.'

Harald, Canis and the Riders of Morkai mounted the saddles of their thunderwolves. Lokyar's Stalkers headed off close behind the Wulfen, a lethal and silent advance guard to scout the terrain ahead and report back by vox. To Norvald Iceflame, sergeant of the Deathhowls, he said, 'Take *Runeclaw*. I want the Blood Claws held in reserve.'

Norvald's eyebrows rose. 'As you will, Lord Deathwolf.' He glanced towards his band, waiting a short distance away.

'They can rest assured that they'll get their fill of enemy blood,' Harald said in answer to the unspoken question. 'But I want cooler heads at the tip of the spear. Some... difficult decisions may lie ahead.'

'They'll understand,' Norvald said. 'The promise of battle is enough.'

'Good. And vox the other hunting parties. Have them converge on our position.'

'Aye, Lord Deathwolf.' Norvald marched towards the Stormwolf, gesturing for the Deathhowls to follow.

The core of Strike Force Whitestalker began its advance. Behind the Riders of Morkai marched the Nightwolves and Morkai's Hunters – Harald's most battle-hardened Grey Hunters. Behind them and on the flanks, giving themselves a clear line of fire, were the Icefangs. They were Long Fangs of the Deathwolves. Veterans and marksmen, though the spirit of the wolf was strong in their souls, so too was the ice of Fenris in their blood. Their judgement was as sharp as their lack of mercy.

The Wolfkin ran along the entire flank of the company. Some packs of Fenrisian wolves ranged further ahead with Lokyar's Stalkers. Whether augmented with cybernetic limbs and jaws, or still in their natural state, they were all monstrous predators. They were the true beasts of Whitestalker, brothers to the Space Wolves but still a species apart. When Harald looked ahead to the baying Wulfen, he saw the line blurred, and it troubled him.

The Deathwolves left the ruins of Rig Delta behind. They travelled fast over the barren landscape. Nothing grew. There was only the rocky plane, broken by jutting outcroppings. Above, the air twisted with warplight, and sigils formed, conjuring madness. They dissolved into howling faces. All were monstrous, distorted, yet they also bore traits that were familiar, as if the souls of fallen comrades were trapped in the sickened skies of Svardeghul.

The Deathwolves ignored the faces. They ignored the attack. They were on the hunt. Nothing would divert their course.

'The scent so soon,' Canis said as they rode. 'A good start again.'

The champion did not often initiate conversations. 'Too easy, you think?' Harald asked.

Canis shrugged, but his eyes were shrouded, uncertain.

Too easy, Harald thought again. An entire world to search, and the Deathwolves were on the trail of their quarry on the first attempt, almost as soon as they had landed. He had followed his intuition, guided, he wanted to believe, by some sound reasoning. Even so, he did not rejoice in the sign of quick success. He distrusted it.

Why have we found the scent so easily? He was suspicious of his own intuition.

The hunt had travelled fewer than ten kilometres when Lokyar voxed Harald that the quarry was in sight, locked in combat with a daemonic host. 'The Wulfen are eager to aid their brothers.'

'They must hold until I give the order,' Harald said. He urged Ice-tooth to greater speed. The rest of Whitestalker kept pace. Soon they reached the top of a ridge, where the Scouts had managed to hold the Wulfen back from engaging.

Harald looked down the slope to the region designated on the Svardeghul maps as the Shatterfields. The land the Deathwolves had just crossed was desolate, but it was a region that had yet to be scoured of its ore. Now they had reached the border of a vast area that had been worked to death. The Shatterfields had once been plains but now the surface was broken by a cracked-glass network of ravines. Between these, slag heaps reared their blackened heads. Isolated from one another, an army of sullen hills stretched to the horizon.

The ridge sloped down to a large plain flanked by heaps to the east and south, and a zig-zagging line of ravines to the west. The ground resembled the cracked, disintegrating skin of an enormous reptile. It was here the Deathwolves found the war. A large band of Wulfen fought an army of daemons. Outnumbered many times over, the Wulfen had retreated to the base of a slag heap in the south. They were partway up the slope, surrounded by jagged monoliths of discarded rock. Their position was strong; the daemons could not rush them in a mass. The Wulfen held them at bay. Hordes of pink Tzeentchian nightmares clambered over each other and the rocks only to be torn apart, each broken daemon reforming into two blue abominations. The Wulfen hurled the new, wailing creatures into their kin, knocking them back further.

'Like Nurades,' Canis said.

'Indeed,' said Harald. The daemonic horde was as varied as it was vast. 'I do not like this unity.'

Moving up through the pink horrors were daemonettes and creatures of Slaanesh. The daemonettes' strides were long and graceful, while the fiends leapt and galloped. As agile as the Tzeentchian abominations were clumsy, the Slaaneshi daemons crossed the battlefield in a feral joy of dance, their song turning slaughter into dark pleasure. They were fast, and the obstacles of the ruined earth could not slow them. They pounced on the Wulfen, trilling their chorus of exquisite murder. Their pincer limbs struck at the throats of the 13th Company. The fiends jumped over the stones, their long stinger tails stabbing through ancient, disintegrating armour. The Wulfen hit back with claw and blade, with frenzy and rage, dismembering and cutting daemonettes in half. Ichor coated the stones as broken monsters dropped back down the slope, dissolving. Yet they kept coming, more and more joining the attack, and they were taking their toll. Severed Wulfen heads arced through the air, raining blood.

Attacks from the air were just beginning. Burning chariots of Tzeentch swooped over the hills. Pulled by shrieking winged abominations, mounted by huge flame daemons, their edges scorched and sliced, while the flame daemons poured wyrdfire over the Wulfen, seeking to incinerate their reality.

'Our brothers stand strong,' Canis said. He looked at Harald expectantly.

'They do,' said Harald. He saw in the 13th Company the indomitable spirit of true Space Wolves. And he saw the unrestrained savagery of monsters.

'If we do not act...' Canis began.

'I know,' Harald said. 'They will fall.' The Wulfen could not withstand the sustained assault from land and air much longer.

Yngvir and his brothers were straining to tear down the slope. Harald did not give the order.

He hesitated. He was torn between two duties – to his oaths, and to his Chapter. He had sworn to rescue the Wulfen. But the more he saw of them, the more he dreaded what their ultimate impact on the Space Wolves would be. And again, there was the ease with which they had been found. The victories on Nurades sat less and less well with him. At the back of his mind, the laughter of Slithertwyst echoed still.

Harald felt Canis' eyes on him. He glanced at the Champion. There was no judgement there. Canis was waiting to see the path the Deathwolves would take.

All Harald had to do was nothing, and this splinter of the 13th Company would cease to be. If the Wulfen were a threat, it would diminish now by this much.

His instinct was to turn away. Against all his practice, against all his history of war, against everything he had been commanded to do, this was what his spirit urged him to do.

Then Harald looked at Yngvir, and thought of the debt his company owned the Wulfen.

His oaths were sacred. The Great Wolf had spoken. This was the path upon which the Space Wolves had embarked. It could not be changed at this juncture. Harald would travel it with all his brothers, and do what he must.

He raised Glacius. He said nothing, and his silence itself was a command. Even the Wulfen understood, and their growls quieted. Then he slashed down with the frost axe.

Strike Force Whitestalker charged down the slope with the Riders of Morkai in the lead. The only sounds came from the pounding of ceramite boots and wolf paws, and they were drowned out by the singing and chanting of the daemons. The horde was unaware of the destruction that streaked across the broken landscape towards it. Fifty metres from the daemonic ranks, the enemy was a wall of unnatural bodies – heaving, writhing, ululating. The singing filled his mind with images of excess and disease. The stench of open wounds, rotten meat and sickening blooms filled his senses. Harald snarled, hurling the foulness from his lungs. He raised his bolt pistol.

Another signal. All along the lines of the wedge-shaped phalanx, gun barrels pointed in the same direction.

Harald fired. So did all of Whitestalker. The air around Harald went dark, the dread light of the warp storm suddenly cut off by the immense hail of bolter shells. The hammering concussion of thousands of barrel reports overwhelmed the daemonic choir. The shells slammed into the mass of pink daemons and they exploded into smaller blue twins. The barrage tore these apart just as quickly. The mass-reactive shells punched through the slender forms of the daemonettes and fiends, exploding their silhouettes.

The Space Wolves stormed into the fray. Moments after the gun fire, the jaws of wolves and the chainblades of Space Wolves shredded the abominations. The Wulfen bayed their challenge, and it was answered by their brothers under siege. Yngvir's pack struck with the ancient weapons gathered from the Fang. Swords as long as spears and axes with blades as wide as a mortal human cut an ichor-spraying swath through the daemons. Harald saw the enemy destroyed as thoroughly as if the weapons had been sanctified power blades. Yngvir eviscerated a brace of pink daemons with slashes of his twin frostclaws. He wielded the relic blades with a perfect savagery. Ichor fountained over him. His jaws were agape in bestial delight.

The Wulfen slaughtered the forces of the Ruinous Powers with a force that stirred Harald to awe. The light of explosions and energy bursts flashed off their new armour. They embodied a terrible glory. However monstrous they were now, they had fought alongside Russ. Warriors from ten millennia past had returned to the battlefield. Their mere presence was an echo of the Imperium at its height.

And of the height of its agony.

Whitestalker took the daemons by surprise. Harald roared with brutal satisfaction as he saw the enemy react with disarray to the attack. Creatures of nightmare confronted a nightmare of their own. The Deathwolves barrelled through the rear lines, spreading their destruction outwards, striking out from the flanks while the front of the wedge pushed deeper and deeper into the daemonic ranks. Advancing more slowly, the Icefangs kept up the punishing barrage of heavy weapons fire. Lascannons incinerated abominations in blasts of searing white, leaving nothing behind but foul ash and dissipating sparks of wyrd energy. Heavy bolters punched through the pink daemons with such explosive force that the shattered bodies could not reform into their blue counterparts.

As if the World Wolf itself had seized the enemy host within its jaws, Whitestalker cut the daemon numbers in half in a matter of seconds. All the Deathwolves joined the Wulfen in howls of war and triumph.

The daemons responded. While their ground forces fell and dwindled, the aerial assault intensified. The skies filled with burning chariots and a swarm of screamers. The chariots flew along the flanks of the Space Wolf phalanx, huge flame daemons unleashing streams of wyrdfire. The Deathwolf advance slowed as the warriors jinked from side to side, seeking to avoid the blasts. Some did not. As Harald and Icetooth raced between two parallel explosions of flesh-corrupting fire, he heard a shout of soul-torn rage, and was engulfed by a sudden cloud of grey ash. The particles that had once been brother warriors settled on his armour and in his beard. Icetooth howled in distress, shaking it off. Harald beat his fist once against the totems on his chest, willing the souls of his lost brothers a swift journey to the land of the dead, and promising them vengeance.

The winged, screaming abominations cut back and forth across the Space Wolf lines. They flew low, hunting together. As if lured by the great spiritual strength of each warrior, they clustered their attacks around a single victim. Their shrieks pierced ears and souls, horns stabbed into the seams of armour and spiked tails whipped in with severing force. Arterial blood shot skyward, mixing with ash and corrupting flame. Heroic sagas snapped to an end as heads bounced off shoulders to be ignominiously trampled to mulch on the ground.

'Now, Norvald!' Harald voxed. 'Tear this foulness from the air!'

Runeclaw roared into the Shatterfields. It flew low, its engines shaking the battlefield. Lascannons and heavybolters streaked fire and destruction over the heads of the Space Wolves and a storm of energy and explosions shredded the flying daemons. The gunship's embarkation ramp dropped open and the Deathhowls hurled themselves down into the battlefield. They bayed their eagerness to be at the enemy's throat and hit the ground running, tearing along the flanks. Half the pack savaged the daemons on the ground while the other half turned their fire on the chariots and screamers. They were joined in the effort by the Icefangs. The Deathhowls' skill with their bolt pistols was lethal, but the impact of the shells was dwarfed by the cataclysm of plasma and lascannons. The air over the Shatterfields burned. It hurled daemons to the ground, their bodies blown apart, their materiality evaporating.

Harald was deep in a maelstrom of annihilation. He and his Deathwolves were the anger of the storm. Abominations swarmed over each other in the effort to halt the advance. They rushed to their extermination. The blue crystal of Glacius' blade flashed through scale and flesh. Every swing was more savage than the last, and Harald poured his fury into the weapon. Every impact and slicing crunch was vengeance and justice. He destroyed with every blow. Whatever his doubts about the wisdom of the mission, his hunger to destroy the daemon was as furious as ever. His charge was destruction made absolute. As he witnessed the supernova rage of the Wulfen, he drew upon it, and his own ferocity climbed to new heights.

The daemons fell, and fell, and fell. They were nothing but meat in the jaws of the wolves of war. Their numbers dwindled. The Deathwolves approached the base of the slagheap. The besieged Wulfen were still taking casualties, but they fought with the spirit of imminent victory. Many of the daemons attacking them turned back down the slope in an attempt to stop the crushing, devouring storm.

They were trying to stop fate itself. They failed.

A pair of flame daemons, caught up in a paired whirlwind dance, rose in a spinning leap from the rocky slabs below the Wulfen's position. Their jump took them over Harald, and just below the lethal barrage of *Runeclaw* and the Icefangs. They came down on either side of Vygar Helmfang. He tried to retaliate, but as he lashed out with his wolf claws, bellowing defiance, his armour and his flesh deliquesced. They dripped from his bones together, a mass of pink and blue-grey and frothing blood.

'Lord Deathwolf!' he cried. 'Preserve our Chapter!' His voice disappeared into the gargling coughs of a drowning man. His beard and face flowed together and poured off his skull. His skeleton burst into terrible growth. Serpentine clusters of bone spurs struck out of his frame with the speed of a scorpion's tail. They plunged their barbed ends into the neck and spine of his thunderwolf. The beast howled with its master. They collapsed to the ground, rolling and fusing into a mass of brittle, self-constricting tentacles and organic sludge. The cries of agony went on much longer than should have been possible.

Vygar was avenged before he truly died. The other Riders of Morkai fell on the flamers, their blades hacking the daemons apart in seconds. Fury unslaked, the Deathwolves attacked the rest of the daemonic horde with grief transmuted to devastation.

The daemonic army dwindled even further.

A solitary screamer flew high above the fray, dodging the fire of *Runeclaw*, dropping lower only for brief moments. On it stood a herald of Tzeentch. Harald only had momentary glimpses of it. The daemon controlled the actions of the army below with gestures and calls whose syllables thundered and hissed at once. The words coiled at the edge of Harald's consciousness, and he could not decide if they were familiar or not. He did not want to believe this was Slithertwyst again. The Deathwolves had destroyed the material form of that daemon fully. And yet... And yet...

It did not matter, Harald thought. Not here and now. All that mattered was the destruction of the enemy.

The air around the herald cleared again, and the daemon reached out to the east, its claws splayed. It pulled at the air as if hauling in chains. From the other side of the slagheaps came a huge clanking of gears, and the pounding of great masses. Over the peaks came four towering daemonic engines. Arachnid limbs of iron punched craters into the earth with each step. Their upper bodies were behemoths of twisted, bulging muscle, devastation made flesh; they were machines of war and they were beings of hatred. Their colossal limbs wielded claws that could crush a tank, and swords the height of a Space Marine. They stuck to the high ground, looping around to the south, then descended, spreading out to surround the Wulfen. The engines stepped over the broken monoliths without noticing their presence. Swords crackled eldritch energy as they came down, cutting through rock and flesh with equal ease. The daemons moved with the majesty of death. There was no rush to their attacks. They were ponderous but inevitable.

The siege was over. The enemy was larger than the fortress. But the Wulfen were fast. They ran at the monsters, dodging the blows, although some were crushed to pulp between claws. One of the possessed walkers was armed with a monstrous cannon. It fired, and the concussion almost knocked Harald from Icetooth's back. Huge shells thudded into the ground, erupting with fire that burned the materium and the wyrd. Wulfen and daemon alike vanished in the explosions.

The devastation could not stop the Wulfen. Their brothers died, but as the daemon walkers focused on their victims, the rest of the pack shot between the legs and leapt up to slash the torsos and arms of the daemons.

The cannon-wielding behemoth reared back. It clawed at the beings who dared attack it. It bellowed like a wounded bull pulling one of the Wulfen from its chest. Ichor poured to the ground in a flood. The possessed walker sank talons half a metre long into the torso of the warrior. It aimed its gun at the lupine blur on the ground, disdaining the two Wulfen stabbing punch daggers into the metal of the barrel.

They jumped away the moment before it fired. Multiple shells surged through a barrel punctured and no longer true. The daemon stalker's material reality turned against it. The shells exploded at once and the daemon's arm and head vanished in the blast. The body weaved back and forth until it collapsed against the monoliths at the base of the heap.

The Deathwolves broke through the last of the daemons between them and the Wulfen. Pink horrors and daemonettes and flamers were still on the attack, but there was little they could do now. The Space Wolves dominated the field, and now they roared over the wall of debris and joined the fight against the daemon engines.

Harald and the Riders of Morkai attacked the legs of the nearest colossus. Thunderhammers chopped and battered the limbs while Harald and Icetooth smashed at a right foreleg. The limb rose high over Harald's head then stabbed down. Icetooth leapt aside as the leg pulverized rock. Harald swung Glacius, and the force of the blow reverberated through his arm and down his spine. The frost axe bit deep. Metal buckled. The monster stamped and circled, sweeping its claws after the Wolf Guard. Iron shrieked, and one of the legs tore away. The daemon stumbled to the side and its aim went wide. Its head leaned forward, a huge, skinned beast shrieking its outrage. Harald met its eyes. He answered its roar and emptied his bolt pistol's clip into the monstrous face.

The shells punched through the daemon's skull. Geysers of flesh shot out the back of its throat and neck. Its roars turned into gurgles of agony. The impacts jerked it backward.

Battle on all sides of Harald exploded at once. The world was fractured by the pounding pillar-sized limbs and the booming of sorcerous cannons. Yngvir's Wulfen swarmed over another daemonic engine with their relic weapons, overwhelming it with their fury and opening molten wounds in its body with their great blades. The largest of the new Wulfen pack, standing on the shoulders of a possessed walker, tore the daemon's head from its body. Two of the great daemons fell. Anger, grief and baying triumph surged as one through Harald's spirit. The events at the periphery of his awareness were sudden and vast enough to pull a small portion of his attention away from the leviathan he fought.

Only a fraction. He never turned from the abomination's wrathful eyes.

It was enough. The claw came in from his left, a blur he turned too late to face. It closed around him and jerked him aloft, off the back of Icetooth. His arms were trapped in the daemon's grip. He could not move. The daemon walker lifted him high. Now its eyes shone with malevolent triumph. Its shattered jaw streamed ichor and its mutilated visage contorted in a snarl as it rejoiced over the downfall of its tormentor. It began to squeeze.

It spoke, somehow forming words despite the canyons of its injuries.

'You will not behold the game's end, Harald Deathwolf.'

Mountains pressed in on Harald's chest. His armour cracked. It split. Blades of broken ceramite cut though his carapace and into his flesh. His fused rib plates splintered. He could not breathe. Pain was a blackness spreading from his core, seizing his consciousness, splintering his thoughts.

'You will never learn your purpose.'

The full length of his frame cracked. He felt a more terrible crushing take place as his internal organs began to rupture. The blackness crept over his vision and the world receded behind a thickening veil. Only the terrible fire of the daemon walker's gaze penetrated it.

The slow, inexorable constriction paused. It relaxed by a fraction. With a supreme effort of will, Harald pushed the blindness away. One of the Wulfen had leapt up and seized the end of the daemon's claw. Through sheer bodily strength and mass, he was holding the arm down and pulling the tips of the claw apart. The daemon walker growled in disbelief. The Wulfen's ancient, ruined armour was little more than scraps now. The muscles of his arms bulged with strain and his fangs gnashed. He was beast far more than human, yet he acted with selfless heroism. Bit by bit, the halves of the claw began to part.

Denial, anger and disbelief twisted through the hollow thunder of the daemon's words.

With a sudden jerk, the Wulfen opened the claws wide. Harald fell to the ground. On his knees, his vision streaking with red and grey, his breath whistling as he dragged oxygen in over floating ribs, he saw the Wulfen twist the claw clockwise. Metal groaned, then screamed, and so did the possessed walker. The Wulfen kept turning the claw. The daemon tried to pull away but sparks and ichor cascaded over the Wulfen and, with the grating of flesh and the ripping of metal, the entire forearm came away. The daemon stalker howled, its black essence jetting out of its stump. The Wulfen turned, spinning, gathered huge momentum, and flung the claw with the force of a meteor into the daemon's head. The edge of the claws smashed the skull between the eyes. A mindless cry rose from the colossus. A sulphurous stench, the death rattle of a volcano, wafted across the battlefield. The daemon smashed the stones beneath it with the force of its fall.

Harald struggled to his feet. He spat blood. His arms were numb, but he had not lost his grip on his bolt pistol and Glacius. He straightened, ignoring the flashing agony throughout his body. The Wulfen warrior howled over the body of his titanic foe. He turned to face Harald. He nodded, acknowledging his debt and his gratitude, and the Wulfen loped away in search of more prey.

Harald followed. He could still raise his frost axe, and as Icetooth came to his side, he waded into the last of the battle. There was little prey now to find. With the great daemons destroyed, the remaining daemons were badly outnumbered, their struggle hopeless. They fought on, as if their purpose had been to die at the hands of the Space Wolves all along.

Harald looked up. The air battle had ended. There were no more flying daemons and no sign of the herald. Harald listened intently, trying to hear past the clamour of final slaughter for the echo of dark laughter. He could not find it. Perhaps there was none to hear.

He was not convinced.

The silence of bloody peace at last came to the Shatterfields. Harald watched the Wulfen of Whitestalker reunited with their brothers. Twice now, he thought, the Wulfen have saved your life twice. The debt is a heavy one, and you thought about leaving them to the daemons.

Yet he felt no shame. He mistrusted the impulse to gratitude.

Twice. Such a great debt. Can this be fate? Coincidence?

More and more traces of a pattern. He could see fragments, but he could not link them. The pattern refused to shape itself into meaning.

Harald looked upon the scene of victory, feeling the cancer of unease gnaw at his soul.

At war, beneath sleep, above death.

I must wake.

But no. The daemons climbing the wall. Leading them, a giant, a vastness of rage and wings. Landing blows in the psychic wall of the Fang.

I must wake.

But not now. Turn the fury against the daemons. The shadow of an assault cannon firing, firing, firing.

The dream-echoes of daemons exploding to nothing under its power.

The giant climbing against the hexagrammic shells.

There is no waking yet.

Only the battle beneath sleep, above death.

The pict screen was black. Vox traffic had fallen into a silence deep as the void. It was as if Krom was trying to communicate with a tomb. He put the earpiece down and looked down at the huscarl.

'How long?' he asked. Around him, the activity of the Fang's augur and vox complex had acquired a troubled intensity. Kaerls struggled in groups at their stations. While one fought with controls, others waved totems and made signs of warding, seeking to banish the disruptive spirits.

'We lost contact with Frostheim ten minutes ago,' said Albjorn Fogel. The overall supervision of the facility was his responsibility. He was an old man, and the skin of his face was like thick leather. It barely moved. But his forehead was creased now with concern. 'Before that, it was Svellgard. It fluctuated in and out of contact for an hour.'

'The problems have been system-wide?'

'Yes, lord. They were so momentary and scattered at first we did not think this was anything more than aetheric flaws in the vox.'

Krom pointed to the pict screen. 'Not just the vox now,' he said.

'That is so. In the last hour, we have begun to experience outages of all auspex readings as well.'

'Is there a pattern?'

'None beyond increasing frequency and duration. When the blackouts end, the vox operators at the other end report no malfunctions with their equipment. They believe we are the ones shut down.'

'No reports of possible enemy activity?'

'None at all, lord.'

Krom worked to keep the frustration from his voice. 'Very well,' he said. 'You will update me every hour of the situation.' He thought for a moment. 'You say Frostheim's silence has been the longest yet?'

'That is so.'

'I wish to be informed the instant vox is restored.'

'Yes, lord.'

Krom left the chamber. He was near the peak of the Fang, and he followed a gallery that led to a turret platform. He pulled back the iron door, then stepped into the howling wind. He looked up through rarefied air into the night sky. The stars were dagger points of cold light.

The cold numbed his exposed skin but could not numb his frustration. Duty held him on Fenris, and the links to the other worlds of the system were fraying. The rise in the incidents had the earmarks of an attack, but it was one he could not counter. There was no provenance and no enemy. As long as the worlds and moons of the Fenris system came back into contact, signalling nothing amiss, his hands were tied.

Even if the news from the system was bad, his oath held him to the Fang. Should Frostheim or Midgardia or any other Fenrisian world go dark, should they fall to enemy hands, the attack would almost certainly be a diversion. Fenris would always be the real target. To break his oath and take the bait, leaving the Space Wolf home world defenceless, was a crime too monstrous to contemplate.

And yet. He stared into the unforgiving black of the void above, and knew that something worse than his most dire speculations was approaching. His fists tightened in frustration. A low growl rumbled in his chest.

He stood on the turret platform for a full hour. Then two.

Frostheim remained silent.

CHAPTER 4

A Symmetry of Blood and Storm

The battle-barge *Allfather's Honour* was at low anchor over Vikurus. It had translated from the immaterium three hours before, holding a stationary orbit over the city of Absolom. Aboard, preparations for invasion reached completion. The Kingsguard were about to descend.

Ulrik entered the bridge's strategium, where Grimnar sat in a throne carved from a single block of Fenrisian granite. 'An astropathic message from Sven Bloodhowl,' Ulrik said.

'Strike Force Sagablade was successful on Tranquilatus?' Grimnar asked.

'They were. They also encountered Dark Angels.'

Grimnar muttered a curse. 'Many?'

'A company's worth. They were already at war with the daemons when Sagablade arrived.'

'So they saw the Wulfen.'

Ulrik nodded.

'The fates have been kind to our hunt thus far,' said Grimnar. 'But the Dark Angels... That is unfortunate. There was contact?'

'Yes. With the Ravenwing. Bloodhowl reports the Dark Angels demanded our Wulfen brothers be turned over to them. Daemons attacked before shots were exchanged. Sagablade extracted the Wulfen during the battle.'

Grimnar's slow intake of breath was as close as he came to wincing. 'To depart in the midst of a struggle is hard. Bloodhowl acted wisely.'

'The Dark Angels would not agree,' said Ulrik.

'No, they would not,' said Grimnar. 'We will deal with those consequences in due course.' He paused, thoughtful. He looked at Ulrik, his eyes troubled. 'A well-timed daemonic attack,' he said. 'I know what Lord Deathwolf would say about that.'

'And that is?' Ulrik asked.

'That it could be interpreted as daemonic intervention on our behalf.'

Ulrik shook his head. 'That interpretation would be mistaken.'

'So I would prefer to believe, Slayer. Convince me. Was the fortunate event chance?'

'It was the chance created by inevitable fate.'

Grimnar's eyes burned in the shadows of the chamber. He leaned forward. 'Say on, old one.' For a moment, he was once again the young warrior eager for the veteran's insights.

'The Thirteenth Company has returned to the materium. That event itself is so great, it has convulsed the warp. It is so great, it cannot transpire without leading to events just as great. The Wulfen come to us in advance of Russ. They will reclaim their rightful place on the Grand Annulus. Nothing can stand in the way of this resolution, and certainly not the Dark Angels. If agents attempt to stop fate, chance itself will be forced to intervene. Do you see?' Ulrik asked Grimnar. 'If it had not been the daemons, it would have been something else. Fate cannot be denied. The abominations were pawns of destiny on Tranquilatus.'

'It is true our course is clear here too,' Grimnar said.

'Aye. The Stormcaller was unequivocal.' The High Rune Priest's scryings had allowed no uncertainty. The Wulfen would be found in the shrine city of Absolom. None of the other strike forces had had targets so precise revealed to them. One after the other, they had triumphed, and Wulfen packs were being transported to the Anvarheim system and the waiting *Coldfang*.

The Kingsguard strike force had had far to travel, and was among the last to arrive on station. The string of successes before immense odds were still more evidence, as far as Ulrik was concerned, that he was correct in his interpretation of the portents.

Grimnar stood. 'To battle, then, Wolf Priest.' He bared his fangs in an eager, predatory grin. 'To battle.'

'Are you sure about this?' Sammael asked. Standing in the antechamber to the astropathic choir of the strike cruiser *Silent Oath*, the Grand Master of Ravenwing stared at the parchment in his hand.

'We are certain of its recipient, yes.' Master Astropath Asconditus raised a cautious hand. The old man was bowed, his gaunt, sallow face deeply shadowed by his cowl. 'Not as to its meaning. The message is open to multiple interpretations.'

'This message is ambiguous,' Sammael said. 'It can be interpreted many ways.'

'None, with your pardon, are good,' Asconditus said.

Sammael did not reply. He looked at the message again. Transcription, already subject to the vagaries of the warp and astropathic interpretation, was rendered even more doubtful by the message's fragmentary nature. '*Leave no sign*,' he read.

Asconditus spoke up again. 'A question? A statement? An order? All are damning, Grand Master. There are only shadows here.'

'And there is no doubt about the provenance?'

'None. It was sent by the battle-barge *Allfather's Honour*.'

The Space Wolves' flagship was communicating with the Wolf Lord Sven Bloodhowl on the *Bloodfire*. Sammael was not inclined to think well of the Space Wolves. For that reason, he was wary of his instincts. He had to be sure of the truth before acting. But after Tranquilatus, he was finding it difficult to disagree with Asconditus.

The antechamber was dark, its vault invisible in the shadows. Even so, Sammael saw light dawning on the situation that had been developing since Nurades. The light was cold. What it revealed was unclean.

The bestial slaughter of the Scouts who had been stationed to protect the Dark Angels' interests on Nurades. The pict from the recovered servo-skull revealing a massive shape with the Fenrisian insignia on its armour. The presence of the mutated beasts on Tranquilatus. The craven behaviour of the Space Wolves, escaping with their monsters during a daemonic attack.

'We bear witness to an accumulation of damnation,' Asconditus said, as if reading Sammael's thoughts.

'We must be cautious,' said Sammael.

'But if the Space Wolves have mutated...'

Sammael shook his head. 'We must be sure.'

Asconditus' voice dropped to a whisper. 'With respect, Grand Master, aren't we?'

Sammael did not wish to be. Whatever he thought of the Space Wolves, they had been fierce warriors for the Imperium. If they had become unclean, the loss would be terrible. The cost of dealing with the fallen Chapter would be even worse.

'What news from the Rock?' he asked. Perhaps new truths had been unearthed, ones that would point away from this dark path. 'Has Scout Dolutas been located?' The survivor of Nurades had disappeared before regaining consciousness.

'Not according to the last report.'

'He must be found!' Sammael said. It was impossible that a Dark Angel could vanish on the Rock. Not by accident. And if it were not an accident, then there was an enemy who had penetrated the citadel, and *that* fact led to its own set of terrible implications.

'There is something else I must ask,' Asconditus said.

'What is it?'

'I have heard that on Tranquilatus, daemons attacked at just the right moment to benefit the Space Wolves.'

Sammael hesitated, but Asconditus' train of thought was growing harder and harder to resist. 'In effect, that is so,' he said. 'I consider that a coincidence.'

Asconditus bowed his head. His silence was sceptical.

Sammael left the antechamber and made for the bridge. The *Silent Oath* was already making all haste for the Rock. The thought ate at him that darker shadows had already reached it.

And that his worst surmises about the Space Wolves still fell short of the truth.

The Kingsguard came to Absolom. Logan Grimnar's strike force descended in squadrons of Stormwolves and Thunderhawks. As the gunships approached the shrine city, they split up, the flights heading for their designated target zones. Each warrior-band had its contingent of Wulfen to help track their kin.

Ulrik watched Absolom grow larger through a viewing block of the Thunderhawk *Helwinter Judgement*. Despite the smoke billowing upward from hundreds of blazes, at first the city seemed almost intact. The glory of its architecture had not been destroyed. Absolom was a shrine city; the placement of every stone had a religious purpose. The veneration of the Allfather was made manifest in cathedrums built for hundreds of thousands, in mile-wide processional avenues of gleaming marble, and in colossal statuary. Many times larger than an Imperator Titan, the statues were both monuments and habs. They were human in form, some robed, others armoured. They were the qualities of the Emperor given solid form. The Guardian of the Imperium, the Master of Mankind, the Destroyer of the Heretic and the Xenos, the All-Seeing, the Exterminating Sword. Before the warp storm, their limbs and torsos had housed tens of thousands. Their skulls were the chapels where worshippers would look out with the eyes of a god, and contemplate a yet greater one. The upturned palms were landing pads, which now received one squadron of Stormwolves.

Helwinter Judgement led its flight of gunships between the shoulders of the colossi. Closer up, Ulrik could see the damage. The face of one statue had been utterly destroyed, and its skull was now an eerie, hollow darkness. Flames licked from the eyes of another. As *Helwinter* flew past, he had a brief glimpse of ongoing slaughter inside the great habs. Mortals were hurled from shattered windows. Things of horn and claw rioted through the fires.

'The daemons have not overthrown the towers,' Njal Stormcaller said. He sat next to Ulrik in the Stormwolf's troop hold. The High Rune Priest glared at the vista of the tormented city. In the rumbling, shaking hold, the air crackled with ozone. Pressure built around the Stormcaller. His rage was building.

'It pleases the daemons to keep them intact,' Ulrik said. He gestured at magnificence turned malignant. 'The place of highest worship turned to unholy purposes.'

'Aye. The desecration is all the more complete.'

'Foulness from within the sacred,' Ulrik said.

Stormcaller nodded, as if coming to a new understanding. 'And the Wulfen are our great hope fighting within the foul,' he said. 'A striking symmetry.'

Ulrik waited.

'The omens multiply,' said Stormcaller. Though his anger at the daemons did not diminish, his eyes shone with anticipation. 'Surely Russ *is* coming,' he said.

Good, Ulrik thought. It was clear the High Rune Priest saw the truth of the Wulfen.

'They shall rise from the daemonic maelstrom as they tore away from the grip of the immaterium,' Ulrik said. 'There is repetition here. The Wulfen bursting through one threshold after another.'

Lower now, roaring through more densely interlaced structures. Arched bridges traced delicate paths through the air between cathedrum towers and free-standing prayer galleries. Ulrik caught more impressions of Absolom's pain. The city's defenders had lost, but some still lived, and fought on. At the peak of one narrow arch, a trio of Sisters of Battle was surrounded by plaguebearers. The daemons of Nurgle slowly trudged up from both ends of the bridge. There were hundreds. The Sisters cut them down with bolter and flamer as they came near. There was space for no more than two or three of the daemons at once. The heroines of the Imperium could hold out as long as they had ammunition, but the stream of plague-bearers was unending.

Helwinter Judgement strafed the east side of the arch with its las-cannons. It burned away a huge swath of the abominations. Then it left the bridge and the struggle behind.

'That bought them a little time,' said Stormcaller.

'Aye,' said Ulrik. 'No more than that, though.'

Lower still. Now the Stormwolves slowed as they made their final descent into the Grand Assemblis. The square was a few thousand metres on each side, the parvis of four grand cathedrums. Statues of the saints were scattered about it, their placement and orienta-tion given the appearance of chance, as if they were living pilgrims making their way towards the houses of worship. They were an illu-sion of calm in the midst of nightmare. Blood daemons of Khorne rampaged through the square, cutting down desperate squads of militia. The mortals fought, but there was no hope for them. They were now only prey for the swordlings, slain for sport.

There were many mortals present in the Assemblis, however, many tens of thousands. They lay in mounds a score of metres high. Some of the heaps were on fire, bodies slowly turning to ash and smoke. Others squirmed and heaved. The dead flailed their limbs as if struggling against a new pain, one worse than any they had known alive. Wyrdfire skittered over the mound, running like water, destroying the lines between rot and metamorphosis. Around the periphery of the square were pict screens. Once they would have broadcast images turning officiating ecclesiarchs into heroes twenty metres high. Now they screamed madness.

The gunships came down into the square. Their lascannons and twin-linked heavy bolters scorched the Assemblis, blasting the land-ing area clear of the swordlings. Assault ramps dropped, unleashing the Kingsguard before taking off once more to continue their purging assault.

Ulrik charged into the square, part of the collective howl of rage. Grimnar led the charge aboard *Stormrider*. The thunderwolves Tyrnak and Fenrir pulled the war chariot, as eager to lay waste to the foul enemy as their master. With a roar, beasts and warrior fell upon the blood daemons. In Grimnar's left hand was his storm bolter. He attacked with such ferocity that it seemed the enemy exploded into body parts and a deluge of ichor on all sides of *Stormrider*.

The paving stones shattered beneath the tread of the Venerable Dreadnoughts Haargen Deathbane and Svendar Ironarm. Daemonic forms vanished in the heat of Haargen's multi-melta. Svendar lumbered forward, a mountain of walking death, his great axe and blizzard shield striking down the daemons with the force of a rockslide. Where he walked, he left a wake of crushed, disintegrating bodies. The crushed forms of the abominations sank slowly into the pools of their liquefying essence.

And there was Murderfang.

The Stormfang *Drakesbane* shadowed the advance of the Kingsguard. Its heavy bolters chewed through the mobs of swordlings, but they were incidental targets. Its helfrost destructor was trained on Murderfang, ready to fire if needed. The Dreadnought's rage was absolute, a thing of shredding madness. The warrior was as unpredictable as a rabid wolf. There was always the danger that the path of its rampage would take it through the bodies of its brothers.

On this day, Ulrik did not believe that danger existed. He followed close behind Murderfang. He saw a purpose now in his meeting in the vaults with Dragongaze and Deathwolf. The feral Dreadnought was himself an omen of the Return, and here he led the charge to recover more of the 13th. Even the Great Wolf followed Murderfang in this charge.

Ulrik brought his crozius arcanum down with exterminating force, banishing the unclean with the symbol of Fenris' spiritual strength. Ichor splashed against his totems. Swordlings snarled, but the snarl of the Wolf Helm of Russ was greater than theirs, and their anger turned to agony before they fell. Ulrik fought with wrath, in the name of what was to come. He had lived so long, and perhaps it had always been decreed that he would live to see these great moments arrive for the Space Wolves.

The return of the 13th Company. The return of Russ.

Events were aligning. The portents were clear. The future was unfolding as it should, as it must, and Ulrik rejoiced to bear witness to it.

The vox speakers of the sarcophagus distorted Murderfang's howl. The rage rattled and shrieked across the Grand Assemblis. The Dreadnought pounded forward, his terrible gauntlets reaching for the sword-wielding Khornate daemons. The abominations attacked, swords clanging against the sarcophagus. They were rushing to their doom, but they were the essence of rage given bodily form, and they could do nothing else. The beast met them with his murderclaws. Blades the crystalline blue of xenos ice crackled as they slashed through daemonic flesh. The daemons came at Murderfang by the score but he tore them apart without pausing in his battering run. He turned to wherever he saw the greatest concentration of abominations. His momentum was relentless. He was a machine of perpetual slaughter.

There were thousands of the swordlings in the Assemblis when the Kingsguard descended. Shortly, only stragglers remained. Then there were none. Daemons shrieked from the galleries and spires of the cathedrums, but the square was purged. The few surviving mortals clustered together, staring at the Space Wolves with awe and caution. Even the ruinous shrieks coming from the pict screens could not tear their attention from Murderfang. They regarded him with terror. They could barely walk, yet it was clear they would attempt to flee if they came within the Dreadnought's gaze.

Deprived of foes, Murderfang paused. The Wulfen of the Kingsguard gathered near him, as if sensing kinship. Ulrik moved to the front of the Dreadnought. The face visible within the sarcophagus was contorted by a rictus of eternal rage. The eyes were wide, glassy, bloodshot, agonised. There was no personality there, yet for the first time in his memory, Ulrik saw Murderfang blink. He sniffed the air. So did the Wulfen.

Stormcaller joined Ulrik. The High Rune Priest's psyber-familiar, Nightwing, landed on his shoulder. It shook its feathers free of gore and cocked its head, training its bionic eye on Murderfang.

'He senses more Wulfen,' Stormcaller said.

'As you predicted,' said Ulrik.

'I have never known him to stop of his own accord before.'

'Nor have I.'

A change came upon Murderfang's eyes. Something more than bloodthirst entered them. There was recognition. Ulrik's soul was elated at that sign of consciousness.

Everything aligns, he thought. The chapters of the great saga unfold before us.

Murderfang and the Wulfen turned to face south, then thundered towards the cathedrum named the Dome of Penitents.

Ulrik raised his crozius and howled in triumph. A short distance away, *Stormrider* followed the feral pack. Tyrnak and Fenrir were eager to follow the baying of the Wulfen. Over the triumph of the wolves, Grimnar's voice called to the Kingsguard. 'Our kin await us, brothers!' He pointed forward with the Axe Morkai. 'Forward! We shall be reunited amid the destruction of the daemonic foe!'

The strike force followed in the wake of Murderfang. The Space Wolves passed between the screaming pict screens, then beneath the towering arch that marked the processional ramp to the cathedrum. The gunships broke away as they approached the entrance. *Drakesbane* and the Stormwolves flew higher. They strafed the open platforms and stained glass windows of the dome wherever daemons dared to show themselves.

The ramp was wide. The golden doors were colossal, monuments in their own right, so that hundreds of penitents at once could pass through them. There would be room enough for *Morkai's Howl* and

Fire of Fenris. The Land Raider and Redeemer rumbled up behind the Kingsguard, tanks of legend adding their ferocity to the hunt.

Murderfang slammed into the doors. The impact threw them back. The Space Wolves stormed into the Dome of Penitents.

Just before he crossed the threshold, a flint of silver high in the air caught Ulrik's attention. He paused and looked up. The gunship assaults sent dust and smoke bursting from the dome. The sky was obscured. He faced ahead once more. He could not shake the impression of having caught a glimpse of something dangerous yet sacred.

Inside the dome, the legions of the Ruinous Powers awaited the Space Wolves.

A space of glittering sanctity had become a cauldron of violence, massacre, sacrilege and madness. The floor of the cavernous auditorium was heaped with the bodies of worshippers, ecclesiarchs and Sororitas. Shrines lay overturned and shattered. The frescoes of the dome had been defaced with blood, entrails and fire. Cherubim had become disembowelled corpses. Stars were now the blazing eyes of warp-born behemoths. Beneath the centre of the dome, a golden figure of the Emperor, over twenty metres tall, still stood, sword raised as if in defiance of the storm of abominations that rioted through the cathedrum.

The sounds of two greetings washed over the Space Wolves. Daemons roared, hissed and gabbled. Plague, wrath, excess and change fused into a choir of evil, a noise damp yet burning, powerful yet diseased. The second greeting was no less triumphant. Howls of war came from high above, in the Celestium Galleries. At the level of the Emperor's sword, walkways cut across the width of the dome, gossamer-thin in the immensity of the space. Suspended on those iron threads and leaping between the archways of the galleries, Wulfen battled daemons. They moved constantly, speed and slashing fury keeping them from being overwhelmed by the flood of abominations.

In the auditorium, the daemons surged forward. Murderfang was already deep into the rising tide. He trampled scampering daemons of Nurgle and the pink creatures of Tzeentch. His claws dismembered sword daemons of Khorne and the fiends of Slaanesh. The wave foamed around and past Murderfang, surrounding the Kingsguard as the strike force charged deeper into the cathedrum.

A vast shape landed before the statue of the Emperor with cratering force and filled the air with marble shrapnel and dust. The walls of the cathedrum shook with the impact. The horned daemon stretched to its full, towering height. It spread its wings. It raised an axe large enough to cut through a tank and a monstrous serpent of a whip. The axe blade dripped blood. Bits of flesh clung to the barbs the length of the whip. The colossus of rage bellowed, and its roar was the sound of worlds drowning in the blood of mindless hate.

It had already reduced much of the Celestium Galleries to ruin. Columns and walkways were shattered. The bodies of Wulfen lay in the wreckage and blood rained down upon the Emperor, streaking his visage with red tears.

The huge daemon strode towards the Space Wolves. Its footsteps boomed. The lesser abominations intensified their attacks. Creatures of the four Ruinous Powers revelled in the approach of the greater daemon, the Khornate abominations most of all. Their infernal cannons fired from the far side of the dome. Burning, laughing, flaming skulls bombarded the Space Wolves. The bones exploded, spreading streaming fire over the hulls of the advancing Land Raiders. *Fire of Fenris'* twin-linked heavy bolters churned the air with exploding stone and fountains of ichor. *Morkai's Howl* attacked with its own flames, sending a stream of purifying fire over scores of daemons.

Ulrik gathered a sense of the full battle in quick, frozen glimpses. The daemon wave was massive. There was no possibility of grand strategy, only the struggle against the nearest foe, survival measured from one second to the next. He buried the crozius in the skull of a blood daemon at the same moment as he incinerated the torso of a fiend of Slaanesh with his plasma pistol. A wall of evil pressed in, reaching for him with claws and talons. Tongues of wyrdfire fell on him, but he was strong in faith and anger. His wolf amulet blazed and an aura of pulsing red and blue surrounded him. The blows of the daemons could not land on him. He waded deeper into the horrors, laying waste to the creatures of the warp. The baying and snarls of the Wulfen fired his blood. He killed with the furious abandon of a Blood Claw, yet he remained conscious of the weight of history on every moment of the struggle. Thousands upon thousands of years had worked towards this battle, itself one more step towards the fulfilment of a greater destiny.

'Strike the daemons down, champions of Fenris!' Ulrik shouted. 'For Russ! For his return!' He howled, and his cry was taken up by the rest of the Kingsguard. The Space Wolves surged forward, feral, annihilating.

Did the daemons before him hesitate before Ulrik's savage joy? Did they wonder at the bone snarl of his helm and the power of his shout?

He thought they did, and well they should. He butchered his way forward, determined to reach Grimnar's side and face the huge daemon together.

The giant came closer, its eyes fixed on Logan Grimnar. It snarled in anticipation. Caught up in the battle frenzy, the Wolf Guard Drengir charged the daemon. Without taking its gaze from the Great Wolf, the Khornate horror smashed Drengir aside with its axe. The Wolf Guard flew backwards, colliding with the statue of the Emperor. Marble, armour and bone broke together. Drengir landed on the flagstones, motionless, and disappeared beneath the claws and hooves of the lesser daemons.

Bellowing vengeance, Grimnar leapt from *Stormrider*, the Axe Morkai raised high, a challenge and answer to the daemon's weapon. The instant Grimnar's boots hit the flagstones, other daemons rushed him. Arjac Rockfist and the Wolf Guards punished them for the temerity of their interference. They cut a swath through the abominations, clearing the path for Grimnar. A new page in the saga of the Great Wolf was about to be written.

Lightning exploded between Ulrik and the scene of the approaching duel. Njal Stormcaller was moving forwards too, summoning an electrical storm, burning the daemons to ash.

A shriek came at Ulrik from above and behind, the high pitch carving the sound from the deeper, deafening clamour of the war. His reflexes responded before his conscious mind understood the nature of the threat. He turned in time to see a burning, airborne chariot pulled by two of the shrieking winged daemons.

A Tzeentchian herald rode the chariot. The pink-hued abomination was robed. In its left hand, it clutched a black tome that burned with blue wyrdfire. Its right hand held a staff whose head was an edged, twisted crescent, the symbol of its dark god. From the herald's chest came a third hand, which pointed mockingly at Ulrik. The daemon laughed at him. It lowered its staff as the screamers angled in for their attack. It shouted in its unholy tongue. Ulrik rejected the words, refused to let them take on meaning. He understood well enough why the herald laughed, though. It was pointing the staff at his crozius. In its form, the Tzeentchian daemon was a hideous parody of his own sacred role.

Ulrik made ready to silence that laughter. Behind him, Grimnar and the great daemon traded blows, Axe Morkai and axe infernal clashing with such force they unleashed blinding flashes of eldritch power.

The winged horrors dived. A coruscating nimbus formed around the pink daemon's third hand.

Ulrik waited until the chariot's infernal steeds were committed to their angle of attack before he moved. At the last second, he ducked low and ran forward, firing a plasma salvo upward. He passed under the winged creatures as his bursts melted through their underbellies. Their shrieks became stuttering wails. They crashed to the floor, dragging the chariot down with them.

The rapid thunder of Grimnar's storm bolter boomed from the centre of the cathedrum. Shells exploded against the Khornate daemon's breastplate. The colossus staggered back a step.

The daemon was raising its axe to counterattack when the upper portion of the dome exploded. Tonnes of rubble fell, smashing walkways. Galleries collapsed. Wulfen and daemons fell with them. Two gunships in silver-grey roared into the cathedrum, heavy bolters and assault cannons pounding the abominations, and descended to where Grimnar and his foe reeled under the rockcrete avalanche.

They were Stormravens. The Grey Knights had come to Absolom.

Ulrik felt his eyes widen. The eruption of the sons of Titan into the battle had the quality of a fevered vision. In the fraction of a second, his reaction passed from stunned surprise to wariness.

Do they know about the Wulfen?

The herald and the titanic daemon looked up as the Stormravens descended. The giant snarled, but the Tzeentchian abomination laughed. The Chapter of the Adeptus Astartes most fanatically devoted to the extermination of daemons had joined the battle, and the herald laughed.

The chill finger of premonition reached into Ulrik's hearts. Dark portents were taking shape before him. He could not see the pattern they formed. He could only tell it was present. In this moment, all he could do was seek to disrupt it by ending the herald's celebration.

Grimnar acted on the great daemon's moment of distraction. Ulrik saw him run forward and bring the Axe Morkai down against the abomination's whip arm. The blade flashed the blue of purest cold. It cut all the way through the limb. Ichor jetted from the daemon's stump. The giant roared more in wrath than in pain.

Ulrik reached the herald as it clambered from the fallen, screaming chariot. The daemon hissed in outrage. Its middle hand, glowing with warp energy, struck him in the chest. Daemonic power encountered the ward of his wolf amulet. There was a flash of searingly black lightning, and the blast staggered Ulrik and the pink horror. The daemon retaliated with a second, more powerful blast from its staff. Concentrated wyrd energy hit Ulrik at the same moment as the giant daemon struck Grimnar in the chest with a massive cloven hoof, smashing the Great Wolf down.

A fist of madness wrapped itself around Ulrik and took him to the ground too, assaulting his consciousness with visions of the impossible and monstrous. He fought the sights. Other pink abominations jumped on him. The daemonic mass held him in place while claws battered at him. Witch energy sought to transform his armour into something weak.

Ulrik heard the shouts of his brothers on all sides. They called his name. They trained bolter fire on his attackers. The daemons were too numerous. They came at him faster than the other Space Wolves could destroy them.

Ulrik felt as if the fell beings would shove him through the ground to the molten core of this world. '*Fenris!*' he shouted, calling upon its icy ferocity. He raised his right arm, hurling back a scrabbling daemon and smashing the skull of another with the crozius. The pressure on his chest lessened. He fired a single shot of the plasma pistol. At point blank range, the burst washed over him. Its terrible incandescence burned into his armour. Damage runes screamed red and blinked out. The purity of the fire disrupted the wyrdflame. Agony cut through the visions. The spell of transformation dissipated. Ulrik smashed the crozius back and forth, crushing daemon flesh and form. He rose from the midst of the nightmares, howling a hunter's fury.

Ahead, beyond the herald of Tzeentch, the Grey Knights had dropped from the Stormravens. They surrounded the huge daemon and Grimnar.

'Lord Grimnar!' their captain shouted. One of his paladins blocked the daemon's killing axe blow with his sword. 'I am Stern of the Grey Knights! I demand your immediate surrender!'

Before Ulrik, the herald laughed.

'You are wrong to exult, abomination,' Ulrik snarled. 'You are already defeated.'

Grimnar answered Stern by leaping to his feet even as the daemon killed three paladins with a single strike of its wyrd-imbued axe. Stern attacked the daemon himself, forcing it back another step with blows from a sword whose power lit the space of the cathedrum with silver lightning. The Great Wolf charged into the fray and buried the Axe Morkai in the great daemon's chest, where ichor from the earlier wound still dripped. The daemon's breastplate collapsed. The monster staggered.

The Tzeentchian herald blocked Ulrik's charge with its staff. It wielded the weapon with two hands while the third held the book aloft. The daemon began to chant. The air snapped. Eldritch energy built up. The colours of the cathedrum smeared. It seemed as though the entire Dome of Penitents was turning around Ulrik, faster and faster, losing all consistency, becoming a maelstrom of stone and glass. The colours interwove, growing brighter, more brittle. Cracks appeared in the air, spreading and connecting. Thin ice was about to shatter. A foul wind blew from the cracks, howling directly into Ulrik's soul.

The pink daemon was opening a portal to the warp.

From a great distance, he heard the baying of the Wulfen. He snarled, becoming one with their savagery. His beast leapt at the throats of his enemy. He brought the crozius down on the centre of the staff at the same moment as he fired the plasma pistol at the book. The staff snapped. The herald's chanting ceased. It screamed. The air screamed. The materium screamed. The maelstrom spin ceased and the colours of madness became an explosion of blood. The cracks in the real became mere scales of illusion, and they flaked away in a storm of ash.

The Dome of Penitents was solid around Ulrik once more. Roaring, he smashed the crozius against the herald's skull. The daemon's body parted with a hideous, tearing crunch. Ulrik sent a plasma blast into the gap between the halves. The herald's ululating babble turned into a duet of pain as the body split all the way, becoming two blue horrors. One jumped at Ulrik and wrapped its limbs around his neck. Wyrd energy lashed down his frame. The other abomination wailed as its twin grappled with Ulrik. It stretched out its arms, seeking reunion.

Ulrik pulled his right arm back, and smashed the crozius into the spongy flesh of the blue horror's head. It reared back, but kept its grip around his neck. It did not see the pleading of the other daemon. Ulrik trained his plasma pistol on the creature's maw and fired a rapid burst. The heat of a sun exploded inside it and its being evaporated.

The remaining blue horror dropped its arms. It regarded Ulrik, its old eyes knowing what would come next. He had destroyed the heralds. This remnant could do nothing against him. The daemon opened its jaw wide as he brought the crozius in for the final stroke of annihilation. He raised his other hand to block the blue creature's attack, but it did not try to seize his fist and the crozius in its maw. It laughed instead.

He smote the abomination with a single, devastating hit, the crozius crackling with lightning, the very anger of Fenris purging the materium of the unclean thing. And the daemon laughed. It burst apart, spraying liquefying flesh in all directions.

The laughter echoed for several seconds after the daemon was gone.

Harald said the fiend called Slithertwyst had laughed too. The thought was troubling. It was a dark echo.

'This is our saga!' Grimnar was shouting. He severed the other arm of the daemon. The monster collapsed. 'Our fight,' Grimnar said, and sent the gigantic head rolling. 'Our business.'

Ulrik marched through the ruin of the chariot to stand with Grimnar as he confronted the Grey Knights. The struggle against the daemons was ending. With the destruction of the colossus and the herald, the rest of the abominations were vanishing under the firepower of the tanks and Kingsguard elements further out from the the statue of the Emperor. The daemons were disappearing more quickly than they were being destroyed, Ulrik thought. They were abandoning the field. They knew they were defeated.

Or else their work is done.

The Ruinous Powers united. The forces of the Imperium divided.

Ulrik saw the catastrophe forming. He saw why the herald of Tzeentch might have laughed in the end.

Stern was speaking of heresy and mutation as Ulrik drew near. Such an old refain. Such a tedious refrain. Ulrik had encountered versions of the same accusations hurled at the Space Wolves throughout his centuries of service. There was nothing new in them.

What was new was the impasse.

'These things came from the warp, and only my brothers and I are fit to judge if these kin of yours are corrupt. They must be handed over to us immediately, as must any others you have recovered. We will see to it that they reach Titan safely,' Stern said.

'Never,' Ulrik muttered under his breath. His pulse beat in his ears. A growl rose in his chest. He eyed the Grey Knights, and faced the inevitable. They were fanatics. They could not be turned from their path. They had come to take the Wulfen. There was only one way to stop them.

'Stern, I'm sure you think you're being very reassuring, but there's as much chance of you taking the Wulfen as of me giving my crown to a blubber-seal. I'd see our brothers dead before I handed them over to be cut apart and studied,' Grimnar said.

'Forcing your cooperation at this juncture would prove costly,' Stern warned.

Even as Ulrik kept his arms lowered, he adjusted his grip on his pistol and the crozius.

Grimnar and Stern were still speaking. The words were nothing more now than the ritualistic prologue to battle. Around the circle, the stances of the Space Wolves were shifting. In moments, the blood would flow.

'I would have thought,' said Stern, 'considering the current situation around Fenris, you would want all the friends you could get, Great Wolf.'

Ulrik stared at the Grey Knight. His limbs went numb with premonition.

'What situation?' asked Grimnar.

Stern answered, and transformed Ulrik's premonition into horror.

CHAPTER 5

Unveiling

The decks of the *Coldfang* vibrated from the snarls. The walls thrummed with feral rage. The roars were growing louder. Hjalvard pounded down the halls of the strike cruiser, convinced he would find disaster at the guard post. The thought made his lips pull back in anger. His pulses were a double-beat of incipient battle frenzy. His skin crawled. His jaws ached as his fangs pushed further out from his gums. As he rounded the final corner, he was charging to attack.

But the barrier held. Vintir was at his post. The door behind him was sealed. The Grey Hunter raised his power sword, but he did not run to meet Hjalvard's rush. 'Battle leader!' Vintir shouted.

Stop! Hjalvard thought. His rational mind wrestled with the beast. *Stop!*

He turned at the last moment and slammed his fist into the wall, cracking the stonework. He breathed through his nose, forcing himself to move slowly, to be still. If his body calmed, perhaps his spirit would too.

He had headed here merely on an inspection. He had almost precipitated the very disaster he had dreaded.

The contagion is growing, he thought.

When he felt he could speak without snarling, he faced Vintir.

'All is well,' he said, hands up as if it were Vintir and not he who had needed placating. 'Have they tried to come through?' he asked. Above all else, he had to keep the Wulfen off the main decks.

'They are remaining below,' said Vintir. 'I think there have been some fights for dominance, but I believe the pack leaders are keeping them in their quarters.'

'For now. And you, brother? How are you faring?'

Vintir grunted. 'As long as I'm not challenged...'

Hjalvard nodded. 'I've issued standing orders. No access to the Wulfen quarters, and no access to this corridor. We will keep the situation contained.' *For as long as possible*, he almost added. He could only trust his coolest-headed warriors to be outside their own quarters now, let alone stand guard on this choke point. He could barely trust himself now.

His vox bead crackled for his attention. 'What?' he snapped.

'*There are ships translating into the system, lord*,' an anxious huscarl said. '*The* Allfather's Honour, *the* Alpha Fang, *the* Bloodfire *and the* Wolfborn. *The Great Wolf is hailing us.*'

'I'm on my way,' Hjalvard said. He looked at Vintir. 'The fleets are returning.'

'Is the hunt finished?'

'Pray that it is, brother.'

The hold below was more filled than the rest of the Space Wolves knew. It held more than just the Wulfen now.

In the *Alpha Fang*'s hololith chamber, an encrypted channel opened to the five strike cruisers. Harald Deathwolf and Canis Wolfborn watched the flickering image of Hjalvard describe the situation aboard the *Coldfang*. The battle leader's every word was dreaded confirmation. Harald grimaced. He had never before felt such pain at being proven correct.

'*We are overtaken by madness*,' Hjalvard said. '*Already seven Grey*

Hunters have fallen to the curse. The transformation has taken them. They are Wulfen now.'

'The mark is upon us all,' Ulrik put in, the ancient voice hard and rasping as a glacier's crawl. *'The change can come to us at any time.'*

'In combat!' Hjalvard protested. *'In the heat of battle! The only struggle on the* Coldfang *has been between brothers! The more Wulfen come aboard, the worse it has become. Tempers are explosive. The training cages are wet with blood. I have restricted almost my entire force to quarters. My ship is a tinder box. It will take very little for it to explode.'*

Hjalvard's tones were harsh with strain. His breath kept turning into a growl. There was a softness to some of his consonants, as if he was finding it difficult to close his lips over his fangs.

'This is what I feared,' Harald said. 'The Wulfen are a curse.'

There. He had made his declaration. It was no longer a supposition, no longer a warning. The danger the Wulfen presented was clear. What had yet to be revealed was the full extent of the threat.

At his words, the hololithic figures burst into static, reformed, and burst again as the Wolf Lords shouted over each other. Ulrik the Slayer's image remained still, dark with intensity. Egil Iron Wolf and Sven Bloodhowl, bloodied from their struggles on Mygdal Alpha and Tranquilatus, sided with Harald.

'Aggression is spiking on my ship,' Iron Wolf said.

'And mine,' said Bloodhowl.

Grimnar spoke, silencing the others. *'The Stormcaller subjected our kin to every test he knows, Deathwolf. I insisted on it. There is no Chaos taint here. None!'* he said.

The image of Ulrik the Slayer nodded once, as if that was an end to the matter, but Harald had noticed a sliver of doubt in Grimnar's voice.

'Perhaps not,' said Iron Wolf, *'but there is something amiss. Some sickness, perhaps? My optic augurs read biochemical hyperactivity in my warriors. Their blood stirs...'*

'We make warp for Fenris at once,' Grimnar thundered, cutting

him off. '*And upon our arrival, the Wulfen will fight at our side. The Space Wolves will defend our home world, and we will do so together! Do you mark that ship that has joined our formation?*'

'I do,' Harald said. The grey hull of the battle-barge reflected the light of Anvarheim with a bleak purity.

'*Our fleet is accompanied by the Grey Knights,*' Grimnar continued as if Harald had not spoken. '*Will you trust the encryption of this channel when the likes of them are present? Will you call our brothers cursed when they might hear? They demand we turn the Wulfen over to their tender mercies.*'

'Then we should do so, and excise the curse from our ranks,' said Harald.

Hjalvard had kept out of the debate of the Wolf Lords, but he grunted now in agreement.

'*No,*' said Grimnar, more quietly now. '*We need them. Fenris needs them. Even the Grey Knights have agreed to suspend their demands for the time being.*'

'*Then why are they here?*' Lord Iron Wolf asked.

'*They have offered their aid. I have accepted.*'

'The threat is grave then,' Harald said. He knew it was, since Grimnar had sent the order to all vessels to return to Fenris. Harald, Iron Wolf and Bloodhowl had already been making for Anvarheim when they received the message. The rest of the Wolf Lords had to cease their hunts and return. For Grimnar to accept the Grey Knights' offer of aid, the crisis must be extreme.

'*Captain Stern's astropaths intercepted a message from the Fang,*' said Grimnar.

'They did?' said Harald.

'*Only they could have,*' Grimnar replied. '*So little was left. Listen.*'

The recording played over the vox feed. The message was garbled and broken. The fragments were insufficient to permit a transcription into written language. Instead, the voices of the astropaths summoned portents through sound. They conjured symbols through the phrasing and tone. That was enough. In his mind's eye,

Harald witnessed visions of storm and collapse, of fire and of an infinity of rioting, inhuman forms.

'And we would bring the Wulfen back with us?' he protested. 'Don't you see, Great Wolf, the role they have played in this disaster? Fenris is attacked while we have been scattered over the Sea of Stars, in pursuit of beings who bring out the most uncontrollable side of ourselves. Will we compound our folly now?'

'*They saved your life, Lord Deathwolf,*' Ulrik said.

Yes, Harald thought. Twice. He was mindful of his debt. Each word he spoke against the Wulfen felt like a frostblade plunging into his sense of honour. There is no debt to the unclean, he reminded himself. There is no debt to the cursed. There was no comfort in those words. Even so, his greater duty was to the survival of the Space Wolves, and he would not flinch from the path he must walk. 'What better way to be introduced to the heart of our Chapter?' he said.

'*You are wrong,*' said Ulrik. '*They are the necessary counter to the threat. If we abandon them, we abandon Russ. If we fight without them, we invite disaster.*'

'*Enough,*' Grimnar said. '*The decision has been made.*'

Harald shook his head. He muted his vox bead and looked at Canis. The champion shrugged.

'They fight well,' Canis said.

'They do,' Harald agreed. *But for whom?* he added silently.

'*There is more,*' said Grimnar.

More? Harald thought. This isn't enough?

'*I am unencrypting the hololith transmissions. Brother-Captain Stern warned me of something else on Vikurus. Prepare to receive pict data from the battle-barge.*'

A few moments later, Stern said, '*You have been speaking a long time under encryption.*'

'*We have,*' said Grimnar. His tone dared Stern to object.

'*The attack on Fenris is not the end game,*' Stern said, as if Grimnar had not spoken.

The electro-missive from Stern arrived. The pict screen above the tacticarium table displayed a schematic of the galaxy.

'*The warp storms associated with your... kin... are not random occurrences.*'

'We never thought they were,' Harald said.

'*You misunderstand me. Their locations are not random. The afflicted worlds were chosen for a reason.*'

The warp storms appeared on the schematic, a disease of whirling sigils.

'*Look,*' Stern said.

More data was added to the maps. With the exception of the warp-struck worlds, the galaxy faded into the background. Lines appeared, connecting the storms. Harald squinted. Even in this form, the pattern was an assault. A coil of tendrils looped from Atrapan to Hades Reach, split to grasp Irkalla and Dragos in jagged talons, fused once more to pierce Spartha IV. On and on the lines went, from world to world, a foul unveiling. A symbol came into being on the pict screen. The image shook. Static ate into the galaxy, though the lines remained strong. They vibrated. They began to pull free of the screen itself.

Then the data feed terminated. The pict vanished.

'*The complete symbol is dangerous even as the most basic schematic,*' Stern said. '*And it is being drawn over the breadth of the galaxy.*'

'What is it?' Harald asked.

'*It is vengeance.*'

'You've encountered it before?'

'*Records of it. No one in the Imperium has seen it for ten thousand years.*'

Ten thousand years. The past again, forever reaching out, forever clawing the present.

'And when was it seen then?' said Harald. The question was ceremonial. In the depths of his soul, he knew the answer.

'It was only ever used by the sorcerers of Prospero.'

Harald reached out to the blank screen. He slashed a finger across it as if he could disrupt the vanished pattern. As if he could destroy the pattern coming into being across the Imperium, and even now devouring the worlds of Fenris.

The symbol was the signature of the Crimson King.

PART 3:
THE RITUAL

CHAPTER 6

Planetfall

Frostheim and its moon, Svellgard.

Midgardia.

And then Valdrmani, the Wolf Moon. The enemy was on the doorstep of Fenris itself.

The system cried out for its saviours. Krom heard. Held by his oath, he could do nothing.

Frostheim fell into its infernal silence, but Svellgard howled before it followed. The vassals garrisoning the World Wolf's Lair saw the seas vomit up millions of daemons. They had a brief moment to call out to Fenris, to give voice to their horror, before they were swallowed up.

Krom heard. He could do nothing.

Midgardia was the inverse twin of Fenris. Where Fenris was glacial, Midgardia was a hothouse. Fenris' winds blew with bone-scraping purity, whereas Midgardia's air was foetid and thick with spores. Fenris permitted only the hardiest, most brutal of life forms to survive on its surface but Midgardia was a lush, fungal jungle, an explosion of life in such super-abundance that it was a riot of all-consuming competition. The population of Fenris was sparse. The people of Midgardia were many. When the warp rifts opened in the air and below the ground, unleashing the daemonic hordes on the surface of the cities and in their subterranean warrens, the massacre was not over in an instant. There was time for the Ruinous Powers to savour their work. There was time for Midgardia's militia to attempt a defence, and so there was time to experience the death of all hope. The population of Midgardia screamed as it was overcome. The scream was the death cry of millions. It resounded across the Fenris System. It was compounded of such horror and agony and fear that it seemed as if it should send the very Wolf's Eye into eclipse.

Krom heard. He could do nothing.

And Valdrmani. Like Frostheim, it fell quiet. There was a different quality to its silence, however. Frostheim went down first, and when the rifts opened across the system, it was clear the ice world had been the start of the attack. Valdrmani went down at the same time as Svellgard and Midgardia. There was only the briefest of cries, suddenly cut off. Or, it seemed, contained. Communications were dead between Fenris and Frostheim. But the astropathic choir of the Fang detected something in the aether of Valdrmani. The silence was tense, stretched to the breaking point. Something was building up, and when the silence could no longer contain what grew, the scream would dwarf all others.

Verthandi, mistress of the astropathic choir of Fenris, came to Krom and told him what was sensed, and what was to come.

Krom heard. He could do nothing.

He patrolled the defences of the Fang. The Drakeslayers stood on high alert, ready to destroy the enemy when it came to Fenris. They longed to take the battle to the daemons, but to where? To which world first?

No rifts had opened on Fenris. Krom saw, in the sparing of the Space Wolves' home world, the lineaments of a trap. The agony of the other worlds tested him. The need to storm to their aid threatened to tear him in half. But his failure on Alaric Prime held him to his oath; he would not abandon his post and see Fenris devoured by the daemonic as the rifts opened, mocking his pride and his arrogance.

He pushed the astropaths beyond their limits. It was the only action open to him. Grimnar and the other Wolf Lords must know what had been heard on Fenris. They had to be recalled. The choir sent out the call. It was torn to shreds by the rifts. No aetheric communication could leave the system. Even vox transmissions no longer worked, except over limited distances.

Impossibility was a poor excuse. The message must be sent. Astropaths died, the blood of their minds pouring from their eyes and ears.

'We cannot,' Verthandi told Krom. She could barely walk now. She was supported by serfs on either side.

'You must,' Krom told her. 'You will.'

When he was not on the ramparts, he stood in the shadows of the stone gallery above the choir, bearing witness to their efforts. He saw the cost of what he demanded. He saw a form of heroism different from the battlefield glory he and his brothers knew. It was no less real. The astropaths were the only active combatants on Fenris. He watched them with respect and envy.

There was no way to know if any of their efforts were successful. There were no messages that arrived from outside the system. There was only the wait for the return of the hunters. The hope they would hear. And the endless, grinding frustration.

Krom waited. He stood fast. And while he kept faith with his oath, the worlds of the Fenris System screamed.

The wolves returned to the fold in fury. The individual fleets had purged world after world in the hunt for the Wulfen. Now they arrived as one, descending with all their might on a single system. Their own home.

But the Fenris System was no longer theirs.

The ships translated from the warp, yet the warp did not leave them. It was here, in the rifts unleashing infinite foulness on their worlds. The fleet emerged from the Mandeville point at the edge of the system. Even with the ships in close proximity, vox communication was growing difficult. Attempts to make contact with the home world failed. Assembling a coherent picture of the situation was difficult. It was not impossible, however. The aetheric disturbances caused by the rifts over the occupied worlds were so severe that there was no doubt where the fury of the wolves would be directed.

'We shall make simultaneous strikes,' Grimnar announced in the hololith chamber of the *Allfather's Honour*. 'The Firehowlers will retake Svellgard. The Deathwolves, Frostheim. Lord Iron Wolf, together your company and the Kingsguard are bound for Midgardia.' Every sentence the Great Wolf spoke resounded in the chamber like the beat of a huge war drum. The Great Wolf's frame seemed to vibrate from the horror and rage within.

Ulrik shared the wrath. No words could encompass the crime that had occurred. No words could describe the punishment that was coming.

The Great Wolf paused. He exchanged a look with Ulrik. The High Wolf Priest knew what Grimnar would say next. All the Wolf Lords did. Their hololithic images were still. They waited for the blow to their pride.

When Grimnar spoke again, his voice was no less resonant than it had been before. If he must make this request, it would be done with power. 'Brother-Captain Stern,' Grimnar said. 'We would be grateful for your aid in purging Valdrmani.'

'*It shall be done,*' Stern voxed.

'*And the Wulfen?*' Lord Deathwolf asked.

'To each strike force, a murderpack.'

'*We risk having our companies consumed by frenzy from within.*'

'It is *done!*' Grimnar roared. 'We will use every weapon and every warrior to reclaim our worlds. Chaos seeks to weaken us. We will counter it with unity. We will not deny any brother the honour of fighting to reclaim our system.'

'Lord Deathwolf,' Ulrik said. 'The Wulfen have not been brought to us by Chaos. They have returned to us to fight this greatest threat.'

'I hope you are right, Slayer,' Deathwolf replied. *'We will know very soon.'*

Beneath sleep, above death, the giant daemon on the ramparts.

Its sword high in hunger and triumph.

No. You come no further.

A duel of thought and dreams and lightning. The sword striking through the echo-sarcophagus. The assault cannon shadow pounding nightmare flesh. The noble savagery of Fenris stronger than the abomination's wrath. The fell hand seizing the daemon's limbs.

The crushing of wrath's form.

The daemon broken, the wave hurled back.

Only for a moment. The wave rising again, and with it a terrible shadow. An echo of a scream not yet heard. It has the shape of doom.

The daemon laughing in defeat. Taunting. Revealing a horror all the worse for its truth.

The silver templars will die. Their death is your end.

The doom gathering definition.

I see it. I see it!

They must be told.

Wake! Wake! Wake!

Two summons came for Krom within seconds of each other. Albjorn Fogel voxed from the augur complex. The fleet had returned. Multiple ships had translated into the system. Contact was impossible, but their radiation signatures and warp displacements were unmistakable. Krom raced from the astropathic choristrium.

'One vessel is unknown,' Fogel was saying. Before he could continue, the second summons overrode the first. It came from deep in the roots of the Fang.

'*Lord Dragongaze*,' Hrothgar Swordfang voxed, '*Bjorn the Fell-Handed is awake!*'

Krom felt the winds of fate howl around him. A culmination was at hand.

'On my way,' he told Swordfang. To Fogel he said, 'Keep trying the vox.' He changed direction, heading for a grav-lift. It dropped him thousands of metres, accelerating to near free-fall in seconds, then gradually slowing in the final minute, depositing him in the centre of the mountain's ancient labyrinth. In the only vault that still held a Dreadnought, he found Hrothgar Swordfang and other Iron Priests, along with a group of Wolf Priests. 'You finally succeeded,' he said. They had been trying to wake Bjorn since Harald had returned from Nurades.

'No,' said Hrothgar. 'This is not our doing. He woke of his own accord, and called for you.'

Krom approached the enormous war machine. The oldest hero of the Space Wolves did not move. There was no sign of consciousness until Krom was a few metres away. The monolith lowered slightly. Optic augurs regarded him, relaying his image to the mind inside.

'Krom Dragongaze,' said Bjorn. The voice seemed as old and deep as the Fang.

'You wake to aid us in our hour of great need, venerable brother.'

'No. I sleep still.' Bjorn spoke slowly. His words seemed to come from a measureless distance. 'I must sleep. There is war there that only I can fight. The threat is dire. We stand on the brink of destruction. You must go to Valdrmani.'

'I am bound by my oath to remain,' said Krom. 'The Great Wolf and our brothers have returned from the hunt. They will drive the abominations from our system.'

'They have not come alone.'

'That is so,' Krom said, startled. 'A battle-barge we have not identified.'

'Silver,' said Bjorn. 'Grey Knights.'

The priests stirred in surprise and anger. Those warriors were not welcome on Fenris.

'They make for Valdrmani,' Bjorn continued. 'They will die on Valdrmani. Their fate will determine ours. You must go, Dragongaze. Warn them. Save them. Save us.'

'I have sworn an oath,' said Krom.

'Break it, or doom us,' Bjorn told him.

'What awaits them?' Krom asked.

The Dreadnought was still. Krom sensed his consciousness recede to a place beyond reach. The vault was again filled with the silence that lived between sleep and death.

Krom realised he didn't need an answer. It was enough to know the Grey Knights would fall into a trap. *Their fate will determine ours.*

The fleets led by the *Allfather's Honour* and the *Wolfborn* entered low orbit over Midgardia. Its atmosphere was thick, forever clouded. The surface was invisible. To the eye, there was nothing to announce its taint. The vox was more revealing – faint traces of human screams mixed with the monstrous howling of inhuman tongues.

Ulrik stared at the cloud cover through the oculus. Anger at the desecration suffused his blood. He was eager to be on the ground. Eager to eradicate the abomination. Eager, too, for the Wulfen to prove their worth, to at last assume their proper role amongst the Great Companies. They would be fighting for something much more than the recovery of their kin. They would be fighting for the salvation of Fenris and the Space Wolves.

The Wolf Lords were increasingly wary of the Wulfen. The spreading aggression was a challenge. What they did not understand, Ulrik thought, was the nature of the test. Fury was in the blood of the Space Wolves. They were stronger with the return of the Wulfen. So was the fury. We must learn to channel it, he thought. We must remake ourselves. Then we will be ready for Russ when he comes again.

'Augurs,' Grimnar said.

'Readings confirm two rifts,' the vassal officer answered. 'They are located near the Magma Gates. One above ground, one below.'

'Good.' Grimnar touched the vox console beside the command throne. 'Is Strike Force Fenris ready?'

'*We are,*' said Egil Iron Wolf.

The last of the ship-to-ship transfers had taken place just before the battle-barge and strike cruiser reached their positions. Grimnar had sent his heavy armour to join the Ironwolves, while Egil's Terminators and recovered Wulfen had come aboard the *Allfather's Honour.*

'Good.' Grimnar stood. He joined Ulrik at the rail overlooking the bridge. 'Let it begin!' he roared. His wrath was a storm. It held and expressed the rage of every Space Wolf. 'Strike Force Fenris, you are the hammer that shatters the enemy's skull. Strike Force Morkai, we are the frostblade between the ribs. Now, let thunder fall!'

'Well done, lad,' Ulrik said quietly. 'Well done.'

The orbital bombardment began. The lance batteries of both ships fired into the atmosphere. The target zone was before the walls of the Magma Gates. The enormous fortress complex would withstand the attack. Anything outside on the walls or on the ground within several thousand metres would not.

Spears of lasers plunged through the cloud cover. The air heated to red. A fierce wound appeared on the shifting, opaque face of Midgardia and fury seared the planet. The attack was continuous. The view in the oculus shifted to display the *Wolfborn.* Along the length of the hull, shafts of concentrated destruction lashed the world below.

We are bombarding our own worlds, Ulrik thought. It has come this far. The pattern has ensnared us this far. But no longer.

With the purifying destruction of these strikes, the Space Wolves were breaking the snare. Dark machinations had created the vulnerability of the home system. The wills behind the warp storms had used the Wulfen to lure the Great Companies away. Ulrik would grant Harald that much. That lure, though, would be the seed of the foe's destruction. No one could use the brothers of Fenris against each other.

This is our trial, he thought. There is yet another pattern at work, a glorious one, and we approach its culmination. We are being tested. We must prove ourselves worthy of Russ and of the saga into which he will lead us.

He stared at the lance fire so fiercely, his vision contracted to the blaze of those vertical suns. He blinked, jolted from his reverie of faith when half the batteries ceased fire. The *Wolfborn*'s bay doors opened. Stormwolves launched. They flew down in formation, their dives so steep they were almost in parallel to the lasers. A new series of short bursts lit the hull. The drop pods plunged into the atmosphere. They too were a bombardment, a living one, and their reach would be far greater and more destructive than that of the batteries.

Grimnar clapped Ulrik's shoulder. 'Fenris has begun its work,' he said.

'It's time Morkai was about its own,' Ulrik growled.

The Great Wolf and the High Wolf Priest left the bridge. They took a grav lift down through the towering superstructure of the battle-barge. On the same level as the launch bays, they entered a huge chamber amidships.

The Terminators of the Kingsguard and the Ironwolves stood along the periphery of the teleportarium's platform. The rest of the Great Company formed concentric rings of Grey Hunters, Long Fangs, Blood Claws and Scouts. Inside those rings were the Lone Wolves. At the very centre were the Wulfen of two companies, and in their midst were the massive sarcophagi of Haargen Deathbane and Svendar Ironarm. The Venerable Dreadnoughts stood guard over Murderfang. He had been subdued with helfrost after the departure from Vikurus. Wrapped in adamantium chains, he was conscious once more. The presence of the Wulfen appeared to have the same effect as in Absolom. Ulrik thought Murderfang was calm, but perhaps it was the patience of a predator about to spring. Whatever the truth, it was possible to bring him here.

The teleportation was risky. Only Terminator armour had homing devices. The Iron Priests had communed with the machine spirit of the ancient teleportarium. With the Terminators' homers marking the full spread of the strike force, the Iron Priests believed it would be possible to send the full complement of warriors into the subterranean warren of Morkai's Gate with an acceptable degree of safety. Most of the complex's population lived below ground. The tunnels and caverns were large. The maps were detailed and accurate. There was no uncertainty to the coordinates. The risk came from the turbulence created by the warp storms.

Grimnar and Ulrik strode across the teleportarium platform to the centre. The Wulfen watched their approach. They dropped their heads before the Great Wolf, acknowledging the supreme alpha. Their battered armour and punch daggers had been replaced using the stores of new, Wulfen-adapted equipment aboard the *Coldfang*. They were restive, clawed hands opening and closing. Their jaws were wide, lips curled back over their gums. The tension of such a large murderpack bled into the rest of the strike force. Ulrik felt the contagion. He could not dismiss it. His heartbeats accelerated. His teeth were on edge and saliva flooded his mouth. His righteous anger over the daemonic incursion lost some of its focus, becoming a beast of its own. He needed to fight. He needed the warm spray of his prey's blood.

He clutched the totems hanging at his waist and fixed his gaze on the crozius arcanum. *This is the trial. This is our truth. The rage is ours. It is mine.* There was no curse here, only the reality of the Space Wolves, the truth of the spirit that had grown larger and more ferocious with the return of the 13th.

'Let the enemy feel our claws at their throats!' Grimnar called.

In the control gallery in the upper reaches of the chamber, the Iron Priests saluted and began their task.

There were pylons at each of the four corners of the platform. They were tall, engraved with sigils holy to the Omnissiah. They curved inwards, their tips pointing towards the centre of an invisible dome over the strike force. The pylons came to life, energy spiralling up their height, building to a blinding intensity at their points. The air grew taut. There was the sharp smell of ozone. The Wulfen howled, their manes bristling.

The shift happened.

A split in the materium.

The eyeblink of reality.

Ulrik experienced the jolt of being and non-being. He was in the *Allfather's Honour*, and then he was in the high cavern before the great underground gates of the fortress.

And the Wulfen were maddened. Maniacal howls filled the cave. The monsters of the 13th Great Company leapt forward, claws out, fangs gaping.

In their midst, Murderfang exploded into violent movement, a thunder of frenzy and war.

In the *Alpha Fang*'s strategium, Harald gathered the Wolf Guard, Feingar of the Coldeyes and Norvald Iceflame around the hololithic display of Morkai's Keep.

'The ship we detected in orbit translated into the warp before we could identify it,' Harald told his officers. 'However...' he tapped the vox. An auspex recording played back. The vox traffic on Frostheim was active. It was scrambled by the proximity of the rifts. Enough was intelligible, though. Dark, twisted voices emerged from the speaker.

'Traitors,' Canis spat.

Harald nodded. 'There are more than daemons below. Our true enemy begins to show his face.'

'Who are they?' Feingar asked.

'Still unidentified.'

'Just one ship,' said Canis.

'Yes,' said Harald. 'They have Morkai's Keep, but we are many.'

'What about the defences?' said Norvald.

'Inactive.' Harald distrusted the new turn of luck, but the readings were clear. Fate was at last favouring the Space Wolves. 'Sensor auguries have detected no energy readings from the gun emplacements. The wyrd stirs in the heart of the keep, but its outer walls are dead.'

'If that is true,' Feingar said, 'the attack must have occurred very recently. A poor strategy to leave yourself vulnerable to retaliation.'

Harald agreed. His loathing for the Traitors did not mean contempt for their skill in the battlefield. They were not fools. It would not do to treat them as such. The assumption that the Traitors had only just taken Frostheim troubled him, even though it was the only plausible deduction. He did not second-guess the augur readings. He had to act based on the information he had.

And he needed to act. The idea of Morkai's Keep in traitorous hands was insupportable. The enemy was forcing the Space Wolves to attack their own fortifications. Harald's limbs thrummed with anger. He would fall on the Traitors and make them curse their own existence. Every second of waiting was indefensible.

He saw the same furious anticipation in the faces surrounding the tacticarium table. The bloodiest, most violent retaliation imaginable was required.

Harald made a claw of his hand and held it above the centre of the hololith. 'We drop into the heart of Morkai's Keep,' he said, 'with the full fury of Whitestalker. They would use our walls against us. So we will ignore the walls. Drop pods first, Stormwolves following in a steep descent, providing covering fire for the drop pod troops. Our primary target is the command chamber. Retake it and exterminate the Traitors.'

There was nothing subtle about the strategy. It was designed as a brutal hammer blow, fuelled by rage. Harald's anger was too great for anything else. So was that of his brothers. The Wolf Guard roared as one, and clapped their fists to their pauldrons.

Revelation hovered before Harald's eyes. He saw the salute as a thin veneer. The truth was the roar. The truth was the beast. He saw the mark of the wolf on all his brothers, and in himself. He saw the division between human and animal vanish altogether. He saw what he had been warning against, and fighting against.

He saw that the contagion had reached him too. The insult of the Traitors was too great. The war anger was too strong. The beast was claiming him.

He saw all this, and then he didn't. The revelation sank beneath the red sea of wrath.

He answered his brothers with his roar, and then he marched from the strategium.

A few minutes later, Harald and one pack of Thunderclaw Wolf Guard with their thunderwolves were aboard *Runeclaw*, streaking through the frigid atmosphere of Frostheim. He looked through one of the forward viewing blocks. The air was clear. Visibility was excellent. He could already see, on the plane of white below, a small shape, barely more than a dot, but jagged, clearly artificial: Morkai's Keep. Ahead of *Runeclaw* and the other Stormwolves, the drop pods left contrails of fire in their wake. Searing claws stabbed towards the fortress.

Harald felt calmer than he had aboard the *Alpha Fang*. The hunt was on, and soothing the rage of frustration. His earlier revelation rose in his mind. He pushed it aside, consciously this time. Those thoughts were useless to him now.

The surface of the planet drew closer and the uniform white acquired texture. The cracks of crevasses and the shadows of mountains appeared, outlined by the reflected light of Svellgard. Morkai's Keep grew. Its blocky form gathered strength.

Harald's calm bled away again. His senses sharpened. The hunger built.

Closer. The distant mountain ranges cleared. The mesa of the keep filling the view. The concentric walls of the keep marking the target.

Strike Force Whitestalker fell towards the silent fortress.

Silent no longer.

The walls of Morkai's Keep erupted with light, the barrel flashes of dozens of guns. Lascannons and vortex missiles struck at the drop pods. The lethal flowers of flak blossomed in such density that the keep vanished beneath their blackened crimson. The huge shells of macro cannons roared through the squadrons. Drop pods exploded, vanishing in expanding fireballs. Other pods had their sides sheared off and were sent into uncontrolled, tumbling falls, shedding wreckage and warriors as they spun.

Proximity alert klaxons shrieked.

'*Turn that off!*' Harald shouted over the clamour. The alarms were pointless now.

In the cockpit, Iron Priest Veigir obeyed. The klaxons fell silent. Now Harald could hear the uproar on the vox. Curses mixed with snarls and electronic shrieks.

'There were no energy readings!' Veigir shouted. 'How can the guns be active?'

'What matters is they are,' Harald said. 'Stormwolves, provide covering fire for the drop pods,' he ordered. 'There is no evasive action to be had. We are committed.'

Straight down, into the cauldron. The anti-air fire was so intense that the sky was a single explosion. The Space Wolves had designed the armaments of Morkai's Keep to annihilate any attack by air or by land, and now it fulfilled its duty. Other, darker weapons added their destructive force to the las and missiles and flak. Wyrdflame billowed and writhed between the explosions. Harald saw a drop pod fall into a concentrated burst of the mutagenic horror. The pod collapsed in on itself, crushing its occupants, then turned itself inside out, becoming a thing of giant, bulbous organs. It continued to change as it fell. It had no form any longer. It was a constant flow of transformation.

The Stormwolves sent out a stream of lascannons and heavy bolter fire. They sought to take out the turrets, but they were firing blind through the storm of flame. The drop pods were in the direct line of fire, hampering the gunships' retaliation, and even they were disappearing from sight. There was only the cauldron, the roil of the air tearing itself apart.

The vox traffic was a cacophonous litany of disaster, of drop pods blasted from the sky, of shells and las punching through the hulls and wings of the Stormwolves.

'Hold fast, brothers,' Harald exhorted. 'We are still hunting! Our claws will tear the enemy from the sky!'

There was nothing else he could do. He was helpless until the gunship reached the ground. He bit back his curses. His fury was indeed strong, but it had nowhere to strike as he gazed at the unfolding of a rout.

Runeclaw dropped below the flak barrier. Morkai's Keep came back into sight. It was unbreached. Only a few drop pods had landed within the ring walls. They were isolated. Their surviving Death-wolves were being chewed up by ground-defence turrets. Beyond the walls, the rest of the pods were spread out across the glacier.

The configuration of the battle changed again. Winged shapes burst from the flanks of the glacier and screamed upward to meet the Stormwolves. They were armour-plated predators, both engines of war and yowling daemon.

'Machine drake!' Veigir shouted.

Angular jaws parted to reveal autocannons. They added their fire to the anti-air guns, flying in towards the Stormwolves on the flanks. Their shells cut across the deadly stream from Morkai's Keep. At the very moment the Space Wolves attempted to change their angle of approach, veering away from the fortress to defend the scattered troops, they were caught in a shredding, interlocking barrage.

Once again, there was no chance of evasion.

The turrets below ceased shooting as the machine drakes screamed into the midst of the Stormwolves. The blistering rate of fire from the six-barrel autocannons pummelled ships already battered by the descent. Vessels that had been the subject of song for millennia turned into meteoric balls of flame. The death of heroes roared over the landscape, shedding wreckage and bod-ies. The squadron turned its guns on the daemonic engines. They took their toll. *Runeclaw* unleashed a coordinated burst of las and bolter, both twin-linked pairs pulverizing the gunship's target at the same moment. The blasts decapitated a flyer. Its head plummeted towards the ground. The body careened off in a wild, whirling spin. It collided with another corrupted flyer, tangling their wings. Both fell, flames erupting from the body and ruptured engines.

Harald punched the bulkhead and snarled as he saw the enemy

bleed at last. Then huge talons plunged through the roof. Wyrd energy crackled around them as they contracted and crumpled ablative ceramite and adamantium. The machine drake peeled the roof back and screamed in triumph. Entwined with that shriek were others, the souls of a crew long succumbed to damnation howled pain and terror and rage. The scream slammed through the troop compartment of *Runeclaw*, overwhelming even the roar of the invading wind.

Icetooth and the thunderwolves howled. They struggled against the harnesses bolted to the deck. Deathwolves fired upward, bolter shells by the score punching into the blue, glowing armour of the machine drake. Explosions rippled along its underbelly. It shrieked again, with anger now, and opened one of its talons, releasing the sheared roof and reaching into the hold to crush the tiny warriors who dared cause it harm. Harald brought up his storm shield and smashed it into the leading claw. The shield's energy field exploded with a rage of its own. The impact jolted down the length of his frame, hard enough for the deck to crack beneath his boots. The talon jerked, momentarily halted, and Harald spun, bringing Glacius against it with a blow to shatter mountains. He severed it and ichor and promethium flooded the hold. Now the flyer screamed with its own pain. The sound ignited the air and a firestorm engulfed the Deathwolves. Contemptuous of the flames, Harald struck again, hitting the centre of the talon, opening a split that travelled up the side of the monster's limb. Energy lashed out in every direction. Fire raced into the engine's wound.

Pain engulfed the sentient machine. It yanked its wounded limb from the gutted Stormwolf, and, still clutching the hull with one talon, folded its wings and dropped into a vertical dive. The sudden shift in mass turned *Runeclaw* over in the air. Harald jammed the storm shield into the torn bulkhead and held on to keep from plummeting through the gap in the roof. Most of his brothers were still in grav harnesses. They dangled upside down, shooting at the machine drake. *Runeclaw*'s engines thundered with strain as Veigir fought against the pull. He slowed the drop, but could not right the ship. Another flyer streaked past on the port side, autocannon shells puncturing the wing and engine nacelles.

The flight surfaces were all but destroyed. Two of the engines had exploded. The gunship's fall was accelerating as the machine drake pushed it down to an annihilating smash.

Bolter shells dug into the daemon ship's plating but it kept its grip on the Stormwolf. The talons were out of reach of Glacius. He could not attack without slipping his arm from his shield and falling from the gunship.

In the midst of wind and flame, the Thunderclaw Kollungir dropped his bolter and yanked off his helmet. His eyes were wide and red and mad. He howled, insensate with rage. The howl went on and on. Harald could not hear it over the whine of the remaining engines. He could feel it though. His blood pounded in answer. Kollungir's jaw lengthened and his hair and beard coarsened. He shook his head back and forth, snapping with lethal fangs, and his face projected forward until it was no longer human – it was a muzzle. He struggled with his gauntlets until they too fell away, revealing fingers that ended in huge claws. He tore his harness apart. Still howling, his body transformed by a frenzy that went beyond war into the most primal being of the Space Wolves, he leapt through the roof. He fell on the daemon's clutching talon and attacked it with stabbing, slashing, biting fury.

The contagion spread to a second Thunderclaw. Leifir ripped himself free as well and followed his brother. As he jumped, Harald saw there was nothing left of the rational in his eyes. He was lost forever to the beast within.

Leifir and Kollungir were flesh. They attacked a thing of metal and wyrd-born sorcery. Yet they drew blood. They pierced the hide of their prey. The foul mix of ichor and fuel sprayed into the hold. Fire bellowed. The daemon engine roared in outrage and released *Runeclaw* before peeling off to starboard.

Two figures fell, clawing at air.

Freed, *Runeclaw* went into a spin. It tumbled and rolled, a ruin in free-fall. The wind at last put the fire out. Harald held tight to the wedged shield as he was thrown back and forth. He caught glimpses of the ground through the open roof. Once again helpless to act, he damned the decisions that had brought Whitestalker to this point, ambushed and blasted from the sky.

We rushed.

We did not stop to think we might be deceived.

We only listened to the fury of our beasts within.

We are falling to the curse.

Twisting, falling end over end. The glacier rushing up.

The engines stuttering, firing in bursts as Veigir struggled to slow the descent.

The world a maelstrom.

Wind and speed and fury.

A sudden, terrible crash.

CHAPTER 7

Nova

Krom stood with Hrothgar Swordfang at the entrance to the Wulfen quarters. Serkir faced them. He held his frost axe with both hands. There was an eager glint in his eyes, but his hackles were not raised. His stance was not aggressive.

'Take them,' Hrothgar urged. 'Use their strength. Seeing them in combat will be invaluable.'

'There are more urgent considerations,' Krom reminded the Iron Priest, who nodded in acknowledgement. Krom would have hesitated to stop here, however briefly, if not for two reasons. The *Winterbite* would not yet be ready for launch. And there was fate. Even now he worked to divine the meaning of that gathering before Murderfang. The Wulfen had a role to play in the events unfolding in the Fenris System. He could no more deny that than he could the coming of winter.

Serkir focused his gaze on Krom. He struggled to form words. 'We... must... go...' he said, the final word trailing off into a growl, one that was not a threat, but instead a shudder from his deep being, a response to the call of destiny. He shook himself, then repeated, 'We... must... go... to Valdrmani.'

Krom gave Hrothgar a sharp look. 'What have you told them?'

'Nothing.' Hrothgar was startled too.

Krom turned back to Serkir. Fate had spoken to the Wulfen too, then. Serkir knew what he must do. His words were so close to Bjorn's. Krom's decision was clear; there was no choice at all. For the first time since the departure of the hunt, he breathed more easily. The fate that had been closing in was here, and he was free to take up arms against it.

Krom made for the grav lift with Hrothgar at his side and Serkir leading the pack behind. They rose to the peak of the Fang. In the final stages of the ascent, the walls of the lift shaft vibrated with the deep thrum of the *Winterbite*'s engines powering up. The vibration became thunder when the doors opened and Krom entered the space dock.

The crew of the *Winterbite* had begun a crash preparation for lift-off the instant Krom had given the order. Anchored to the dock, the Nova-class frigate was small and light as warships went. It was still a mountain tethered to another. It rumbled now like a volcano on the verge of eruption. It too was eager for the battle to be joined.

Waiting for Krom were the warriors of Fierce-eye's finest. They had assembled as soon as Krom had given the order for mobilisation: Beoric Winterfang and the Wolf Guard in terminator armour, Hengist Ironaxe at the head of the Grey Hunters, Egil Redfist and his Blood Claws. They were the elite of Krom's Great Company. They were a pack of hunters hungry for war. The icon of the sun wolf on their pauldrons seemed to snarl in frustration at having been held back so long.

'The Great Wolf has unleashed us?' Beoric asked.

'No,' said Krom. 'He has returned, but we still have no contact. Bjorn the Fell-Handed sends us to the rescue of the Grey Knights.'

'*What?*' said Egil, astounded.

'They are heading into a trap on Valdrmani,' Krom told him. 'If they fall, our Chapter will suffer a mortal blow.' With that he crossed the dock at a fast march, past vassals and servitors completing the final tasks before the launch. He strode up an embarkation ramp into the mustering bay of the *Winterbite*. The ramp rose behind the last of the warriors, slamming shut with a reverberating clang.

'Beoric and Hengist, you are with me on the bridge. The rest of you, remain here with our brothers of the Thirteenth Company. The journey will be brief. Action will be immediate.'

'Shipmaster,' he voxed as he strode from the bay. 'We are aboard. Is the ship ready?'

'*Just now, lord.*'

'Then launch.'

He broke into a run. He felt the power of the engines run through the halls of the frigate like fire through his blood. The decks trembled, then his weight multiplied, g-force pressing down as the ship hurled its great mass towards the sky. Krom did not slow. He and his brothers charged towards the bridge as if reaching it would bring them to their target sooner.

The *Winterbite* did not have far to travel. Merely the distance from Fenris to its moon. But Krom had been conscious of time flowing away from the moment Bjorn had returned to the silence of his war beneath sleep. No seconds had been wasted. The frigate had departed the moment it could. But for every one of those seconds, the Grey Knights had drawn closer to Valdrmani, and none of the hails from Fenris had been answered.

The Grey Knights could not be warned. The only hope was that they could be stopped.

Not enough time, Krom thought. Not enough. It was as if he could picture the Grey Knight ship knifing through the system, approaching the moon while he still had not left the upper atmosphere of Fenris.

He burst onto the bridge. The oculus showed the void and the face of Valdrmani. Already the moon was visibly growing closer. Its fall into silence had been a special torture for Krom. There were hundreds of thousands of citizens in the Longhowl domeplex. They were on the threshold of Fenris. Krom should have been able to reach out from the peak of the Fang and strike at the daemonic foe.

'How close are the Grey Knights?' he demanded.

The augur officer looked up. 'They have already arrived.'

No time.

The distress call was clear now. The signal the astropaths of Titan had so painfully pieced together from the shreds that escaped the warp was whole. Precise, focused, it came from Valdrmani, not Fenris, broadcast from Longhowl. The cry went out on sub-warp frequencies too. When Stern switched to its channel on the vox, he could listen to the full message. He did so again as he boarded the Stormraven *Deimos Glaive.*

'They're still calling?' Brother-Librarian Carac asked. The shadow of his psychic hood accentuated the angles of his long, sharp features.

'They are.'

'It isn't automated?'

'No.' Stern drew the grav harness over his shoulder. 'The words repeat, but there are variations in the voice.' It was hoarse, exhausted, sometimes almost inaudible.

'Don't they see us?' said Xalvador.

'The speaker is not a Space Wolf,' said Stern. 'These are mortals. I doubt they will believe in their salvation until it is upon them. So let us be about it.'

The Stormravens launched. They shot away from the bays of the battle-barge. Below, Valdrmani awaited. Stern knew that Chaos rioted on the moon, though it presented a face of emptiness and silence. The surface was a desert of red dust, never to be moved by a wind. There was no atmosphere. The domes of Longhowl became clear.

'No breaches,' Carac said.

'So it would seem,' said Stern.

There was no vapour of escaping air from the domes. Their forms were intact.

'Strange the daemons should take such care,' Carac mused.

'Deaths by sudden cold and asphyxiation are too merciful to be enjoyed,' Stern said. 'If the incursion began inside Longhowl, the enemy would not need to force an entry.'

Even as he spoke, his answer dissatisfied him. Another reason came to him in the next heartbeat. If there were corrupted mortals in the enemy ranks, they would need air. And if that were true...

The signal, he thought.

In that moment, the signal changed. It became a single word.

'*Welcome*,' the voice said.

Then it laughed. Well it might. The subterfuge had been perfect. In an instant, Stern beheld the enormous implications of what had been done. The enemy had simulated a broken distress call that had passed every test of authenticity the Grey Knights had used on it. Worse, he now saw dire purpose in the fact that *only* the Sons of Titan had succeeded in intercepting it. The signal had been imperceptible to the Space Wolves because it had been aimed specifically at the Grey Knights.

The Space Wolves were not countering the enemy's plan by returning to the Fenris system. They were fulfilling it, lured by means of the Grey Knights to arrive at the appointed time.

We were lured too, Stern thought. The enemy wants us here.

Now.

At this very spot.

The laughter became a maniacal howl. The signal cut out.

In the centre of Longhowl was a huge cylindrical tower. It stood higher than any of the domes. It split open, revealing the barrel of an immense gun.

The nova cannon fired.

Destruction had a royal majesty. The eternal night of Valdrmani exploded into ruby-coloured day. A multitude of energy columns shot out of the barrel at once. They lanced into the void, and into the core of the Grey Knights vessel sitting in low orbit.

The battle-barge was still fully visible through the Stormravens' viewing blocks. Now it was lit by the terminal beam. Stern watched the display in horror. He watched annihilation unfold in silent grace.

The light seared so brightly, it seemed to burn the void itself. It sliced through the battle-barge from underbelly to superstructure. The ship held its form for a long, slow moment that was less than the single beat of a heart, then the bow began to dip. The stern moved forward.

The battle-barge became two. The light between its identities expanded, becoming brighter yet, becoming the cry of plasma, the wail of a sun's birth and of a sun's death. The shockwave rippled over the length of the vessel. The wave travelled outwards. It reached Valdrmani. The Stormravens were beyond its greatest force. Even so, it hammered them with its passage. The engines of *Deimos Glaive* howled in protest. A great fist shook the gunship, blurring the view of the battle-barge, then passed. The fire from the heart of the ship blossomed. It swallowed the halves before they could begin to tumble. They disintegrated in its jaws. The light hurled the pieces away.

A monstrous dawn flared over the face of Valdrmani, then faded. The nova cannon ceased fire and night returned, illuminated by a sombre fireball in the heavens. And then the rain came. The broken, burning pieces of the vessel began their fall to the surface. Flung with the force of the battle-barge's death, many streaked moonwards at immense velocity. They were comets of broken vaults, vast marble columns becoming broken spears, meteors of adamantine slag. A head ten metres across, from the bow's statuary, smashed through *Bane of the Magi*. The gunship exploded, becoming more of the rain of wreckage.

The domeplex would survive. It was designed to withstand such impacts. The Stormravens were not.

'Get us down!' Stern ordered. He stared at the domes, willing the gunships to descend faster. The Grey Knights were exposed to the hurtling debris of their ship. Longhowl would give them the necessary shelter.

And the even more vital chance at revenge.

* * *

The Wulfen leapt towards Ulrik and Grimnar. They were a mass of fangs and blades. They were larger than any other Space Wolf. Ulrik saw what only their enemies had witnessed until now. The utter madness of violence coupled to an unparalleled physical force of war. The Wulfen were a fury that could not be stopped.

Ulrik did not blink. He kept faith with the 13th Company.

The Wulfen leapt over his head. Murderfang stormed after them, his vox speakers shrieking, overloaded by the howling insanity within. On instinct, Ulrik and Grimnar moved aside to let him pass.

Two seconds had passed since the teleportation.

The last of the disorientation leaving him, Ulrik turned in the direction of the Wulfen charge. They had passed through the ranks of Strike Force Morkai like a clawed wind.

'They are frenzied,' said Grimnar.

'The teleportation process,' Ulrik surmised. There was nothing but the animal in them now. Yet they knew the enemy, and fell upon the abominations.

The Space Wolves had arrived on target. The cavern was the grand entrance to the underground settlements of Midgardia. Behind, the ground sloped gradually back up to the surface. Ahead, huge iron doors engraved with the two heads of Morkai opened onto the warren of tunnels. From the dark within came daemons. The unholy unity that had prevailed upon the other worlds beset by the warp storms held true here – daemonettes, plaguebearers, pink horrors and the swordlings rushed out together. The Wulfen tore into them before the first Terminator opened up with storm bolters.

Two seconds, that was all. Then the rest of Strike Force Morkai joined the assault.

The fire of the Wulfen was among them all. Ulrik felt it in his blood and in his bones. As he drove a plaguebearer's head between its shoulders, he could feel the pull to the feral, stronger than it had ever been. His jaws ached as his fangs sought to push out from his gums. Every breath was a snarl.

'The gift is upon us, brothers!' he shouted. 'Rejoice! We are among the blessed of Russ!'

The flood of daemons was immense. They attacked with a lethal unity. The speed of the daemonettes and blood daemons was a distraction, demanding a response to their attack while the plague-bearers closed in with inexorable patience to deliver their heavy blows. The pink horrors kept their distance. They hurled sorcerous bolts into the fray. Mutating light struck the Space Wolves.

Brothers died. Some went down to scores of wounds inflicted by blade or claw. Others collapsed with their lungs foaming out of their mouths and nostrils. And there were those who succumbed to the mutagenic fire. Their armour became a gnawing cartilage. Their flesh became a vortex of change that ended only with death, when it slid off their skeletons to pool on the cavern floor.

Ulrik heard the cries of sagas cut short. And he raged.

Far more sagas grew longer in deed and glory. For every brother who fell, dozens of daemons were rent asunder, blown apart and crushed. The battle was ferocious. It was also brief. His armour covered in ichor, his breath turning into a snarl, Ulrik suddenly found there were no more abominations to destroy. The cavern was awash with foulness. Bodies lay in heaps. Their forms were slowly melting into nothing.

Inhuman whispers and babbling came from deeper in the tunnels. The Wulfen and Murderfang were about to run through the doors after their prey.

'*Halt!*' Grimnar roared.

The Wulfen stopped in their tracks. The slaughter of the daemons had eased the confusion caused by the teleportation. Killing was something they understood, and this had been a good hunt. Ulrik saw traces of rationality return to them. They bowed to Grimnar. Murderfang, still under the influence of their presence, waited also. Unintelligible mutters growled from his vox speakers.

'The enemy is on the run, Great Wolf,' Njal Stormcaller said.

'And we will keep him running. Our wait will be short.'

Volkbad Wulftongue stepped forward. 'Indeed,' he said. 'I am in vox contact with elements of the defence forces. The Midgardians are coming to join us.' The leader of the Shieldbrothers spoke approvingly. The Terminator pack dwarfed any mortal, but they could appreciate valour even in that humble form.

'They are still fighting?' Ulrik asked.

'Barely. What remains of their units are converging on this point.'

The mortals arrived a few minutes later. Some found their way down from the surface. Most came from the tunnels. They were ragged from battle. Their uniforms were torn and caked in mud, dust and blood, and their eyes were haunted. They had beheld sights no mortal should even imagine.

Their exhaustion fell away as they entered the Space Wolves' presence. Their determination was renewed, though they gazed fearfully at the Wulfen.

While the mortals gathered, forming themselves into something like squads, Grimnar spoke over the vox with Egil Iron Wolf. Several times, Ulrik heard him ask the Iron Wolf to repeat himself. Communications were going to be difficult even over these relatively short distances.

When Grimnar was done, he asked Wulftongue, 'Are you able to track the teleportation homers on the surface?'

'There are some fluctuations of the signal,' Wulftongue said. 'It is strong enough for now.'

Grimnar nodded. 'Well enough,' he said. He raised his voice to speak to the full company. 'Strike Force Fenris has taken the Magma Gates,' he announced. 'The Iron Wolf is ready to advance. Now we will reclaim Midgardia. As above, so below. We advance together, scouring each zone of the abomination. The daemon will find no refuge, nowhere to regroup. Brothers, *to war!*'

With those words, he loosed the Wulfen. They ran into the tunnels, Murderfang close behind. The tunnels were barely wide enough for the passage of a Dreadnought, and his roars were bounced around the narrow stone confines, echoing ahead, a horn blast of doom.

The Space Wolves followed. Past the doors, there were three tunnel entrances. Rather than reduce the effectiveness of the company
by restricting his warriors in tight confines, Grimnar divided the
strike force between the three passages.

'All must be cleansed,' he declared.

Ulrik moved with Grimnar and his Wolf Guard down the central tunnel. He was one step behind the Great Wolf, ahead even of
his champion, Arjac Rockfist. The Wulfen were howling much further ahead. *Ulrik needs to have them in his sight. He needed to
bear witness.*

They encountered no daemons for the first hundred metres, only
their bodies, shredded by the Wulfen. Then the tunnels branched
again. And then again. And again. At each intersection, Grimnar
divided the strike force further. The smaller squads could advance
more quickly. The Space Wolves spread through the caverns of Midgardia. The great scouring had begun.

Daemons lurked in the darkness. They attacked from the shadows,
lunging out from side passages, ventilation shafts and crevasses in
the walls and cave roofs. They were scattered. They stood no chance.
Flamers, bolters, thunderhammers and the Stormcaller's conjured
lighting burned them to ash or smashed them to pulsing flesh in
pools of ichor. They barely slowed the advance.

'Where are they all?' Arjac asked as he smashed a plaguebearer
against a wall with Foehammer. The daemon slid to the ground,
its upper torso and skull turned to mush. 'Not all at the surface, I
hope. No sport in that.' The Man-Mountain marched by himself just
behind Grimnar. His huge frame filled most of the tunnel.

'They will be closer to the habitation zones,' Ulrik said. 'Where
there is prey.'

The tunnels thus far were access routes, exhausted mining seams,
and maintenance shafts. The few larger caverns the Space Wolves
had passed were warehouses and turbine rooms where huge fans
created wind for the underworld, circulating the air. They had
seen a few mutilated remains, but very few signs of the citizens of

Midgardia. Ulrik presumed they had sought shelter in their homes. Concentrated together, they would have presented desirable targets for the daemons – so many victims, so many to suffer and to see others suffer in turn.

Massacres that would now be avenged.

More tunnels, more divisions, more speed. The Wolf Guard caught up to a pack of Wulfen. Daemons appeared and died in seconds.

Hours into the advance, Ulrik heard Grimnar call Egil Iron Wolf's name several times, then curse.

'What news?' Ulrik asked.

'None now,' Grimnar said. 'Not for some time.' He cursed.

'They were advancing well.' The Iron Wolf's forces were moving entirely in armoured vehicles. The mist at the surface was so corrosive it could dissolve armour.

'Until they reached a swamp. The daemons have been hitting them hard.'

'They can't free the tanks?'

'This is what I hoped to learn. I've heard nothing for almost an hour. In his last vox transmission, the Iron Wolf was cursing about spores eating through armour and flesh. Now he doesn't answer. We have no vox contact with the surface.'

'How far have we come without their cover?' Ulrik asked. If the tandem advance had broken down, Strike Force Morkai would be much more exposed to a counter attack.

'Wulftongue has lost the signal,' said Grimnar. 'We cannot tell where Strike Force Fenris is.'

'If we purge...' Ulrik began. He was interrupted by the angry growls of the Wulfen. 'The enemy is close,' he said.

They heard the daemons before they saw them. There was a rasping sound, as though the tunnels had begun to breathe. The noise grew louder, becoming the skittering of claws, the dragging of blades, the snarls and chanting of thousands of abominations. A great tide was coming in from all directions.

The tunnel ahead of Grimnar's squads curved to the left. The air filled with a cloying odour. It worked its way through the rebreather of Ulrik's helm, reaching behind his eyes. It sought to lull him. It invited him to lay down arms and surrender to a dream of excess. He snarled, shaking free of the unclean illusion. The Wulfen howled and raced forward, enraged by the malevolent scent.

Grimnar raised the Axe Morkai. 'Rend the abomination limb from limb!' he shouted. The Space Wolves charged as one. They rounded the corner and barrelled into a huge cluster of Slaaneshi fiends. The daemons lashed out with pincers and stingers and ceiling vents disgorged flamers. They fell in the midst of the Space Wolves, the fire of change washing over the warriors.

Bells began to toll. From behind came the monotone chants of the plague daemons. They hacked at the Grey Hunters bringing up the rear. Fell blades cut through ceramite. Disease ate at the souls of heroes.

The Space Wolves hit the daemons with fire and blade. The Wulfen cut abominations in half with single blows of their relic weapons. Mounted on their backs, the stormfrag auto-launchers responded to the neural impulses of the Wulfen. The grenade explosions were huge in the tunnel. They blasted craters of flesh, splashing the cavern walls with wet, broken chunks of daemon.

A daemon dropped in front of Ulrik. His momentum carried him through the full burst of its wyrdflame. Change seized him. It sank claws into his being and sought to remake him. It fought with another force of transformation. The gift of the Wulfen was there. He felt the beast rage against the daemonic influence. Its hold on his soul was deeper. The flames could not touch him. He retaliated with a different flame, incinerating the form of the daemon with plasma.

The wrath of wolves overwhelmed the plague of daemons. Grimnar's squads stormed over and through the enemy. The more daemons there were, the more prey there was. The advance did not slow. It accelerated. A cleansing flame of bestial rage swept through the tunnel.

Ulrik emerged from the wave of daemons covered in ichor. He

paused for a moment to take in the state of his brothers. There had been losses, and there were serious injuries. These were only fuel for anger. Terminators and Wulfen thundered on. On the squad channels, Ulrik heard how easily breathing turned to growls. The gift was growing stronger. So were the warriors.

He ran on forward again, catching up to Grimnar. 'The spirit of the wolf burns high in our brothers,' he said. 'We cannot be stopped.'

The Great Wolf's face was grim. 'I fear the Iron Wolf has been, or worse,' he said. 'The daemons have had the opportunity to mass a counter attack.'

'What of the rest of Strike Force Morkai?'

'Stymied, I think. I cannot reach all of them. Those who answer cannot yet break through the ambushes.'

'So only we are advancing.'

Grimnar nodded. 'So it would seem. We strike on,' he said. 'We will plunge our claws into the enemy's heart and rip it out.'

'The others will triumph too.'

'They will,' Grimnar affirmed. He growled with such conviction, it seemed to Ulrik the words themselves had the power to shape reality.

Though the tunnels continued to branch, Grimnar no longer divided the force. The squads plunged down the larger passages. Here they had liberty of movement along with the power to smash the foe. The daemons attempted repeated ambushes. They were torn to pieces for their pains.

The temperature climbed as the Space Wolves moved deeper and deeper underground. They reached settlements built into large caverns. Streams of lava flowed across the floors and interconnected walkways and living platforms hung from the ceilings. The people of Midgardia had lived inside their forges, suspended above a killing heat and had braved molten death the way the people of Fenris confronted the cold. The mining and manufacturing communities were small. Each had been home at most to a few thousand. They were all empty now, broken tombs. Pieces of bodies littered the platforms. Flesh without bones was draped across thresholds and hung from windows. Flayed skeletons were suspended from metal frameworks, still dripping blood. They were coated with oozing, viscous slime and buzzed with otherworldly insects. The metalwork on the walls of the suspended habs had been defaced and the engravings of wolf heads and hammers had been gouged by claws. The new markings formed runes that writhed in the corner of the eye.

The deeper the Space Wolves went, the worse and more elaborate the desecrations became. Bodies were fused together into altars of bone. On the central platform of one settlement, a dozen mortals had been assembled into a single rune. Ulrik smashed the sculpture as he marched past. The violence he did to the dead was a necessary evil to free their souls of these new, cursed bonds.

He could not read the runes. No human could without suffering moral damage. Even so, the traces of meaning scraped at the edge of consciousness. The same four runes kept repeating. These were names. Their frequency was increasing, as was their size, as if the names were being shouted louder and louder.

A summoning.

'We are seeing pieces of a ritual,' he told Grimnar.

'Ongoing?'

'It has been completed,' Stormcaller answered. 'The energy of the wyrd is present, but fading. Something grave has already transpired.'

They went through more settlements, deeper beneath the ground, the air wavering in the heat, the tunnels flickering orange, lit by lava now always close at hand. There were more ambushes. The daemons attacked now at wherever the passages were at their narrowest and movement most restricted.

There was blood. Brothers fell. But so did each wave of abominations, utterly extinguished.

Settlement 529 was larger than the others the Space Wolves had traversed, though it too occupied a single cavern. A fallen sign by the access walkway read *Deepspark*. The citizens had given 529 a name. There were none now to speak it. The community was another grave. There were fewer bodies here and none were intact. All were burned, as if the cavern had become a giant crematorium.

The Wulfen moved cautiously along the wide metal walkway. They growled warnings, their hackles up. There was no threat visible, but Ulrik could feel the imminence of presence. Something pressed hard on the air, stretching the membrane of reality.

'The foe is close,' Stormcaller said.

'From what direction?' Grimnar asked.

'I cannot tell. From the wyrd.'

Ulrik glanced over the railing of the walkway at the floor of the cavern. He hissed at what he saw.

'That is why,' he said, and pointed. The lava channels had been altered. They had become the four runes. Molten rock flowed through unholy names.

'The four runes are joined,' Stormcaller said. 'Four names have become one. We approach the heart of Midgardia's torment. The great powers of Chaos have united. The hordes we are fighting are commanded by a unity of daemon lords.'

'Then their destruction will be Midgardia's liberation,' said Grimnar. 'Do you hear, craven scum?' he bellowed. 'The sons of Fenris have come to rip you from this realm! You do well to hide, but do not think you will escape us!'

The squads reached the centre of Deepspark. The platform was large and had acted as a town square. A chapel to the Allfather and hall of sagas were built on opposite sides. Walkways and metal suspension bridges converged onto it, creating a nexus point in the web of iron paths.

The membrane tore.

Warp rifts opened up over four major walkways. Behind the Space Wolves and ahead, to the left and the right, reality wailed and disgorged a legion of abominations. This was more than an ambush. Daemons bounded and lurched over the bridges, clamouring for the blood of heroes.

Four hordes. Four armies of the Ruinous Powers. Towering over each were four princes. The rifts tore wider at their arrival and the cavern trembled with the sounds of their names, becoming a volcanic fanfare. Lava erupted from the runes. Tongues of rock licked up towards the walkways. The edges of the channels contorted into lips. Grinding voices paid tribute to the forces that gave them life.

Mordokh.

Arkh'gar.

Tzen'char.

Malyg'nyl.

The names were attacks. Each syllable stabbed behind Ulrik's eyes. And though he had escaped the meaning of the runes, their constant repetition had left its residue on him. When the names sounded like the tolling of granite bells, he knew what they were. He knew the daemons. They insisted upon it. They marched to collect their choice prey, and they would have their victims die in the knowledge of what great being had brought them low.

Grimnar laughed. He raised the Axe Morkai with both hands. It flashed with its own wyrd energy, hungry to punish the daemons with the same force that embodied them.

'Good sport at last, brothers!' he roared. 'For Russ! For Fenris!'

'*For the wolftime!*' came the answer. It turned into a howl that shook the cavern to its roots. From vox speaker and bestial throat, the howl went on and on.

Rage and animal hunger were one.

Ulrik rode the fury of the gift. Its fire consumed his thoughts. At the Great Wolf's side, amidst brothers who had fought for ten thousand years, he charged towards the princes of damnation.

Anger. Instinct. Reason.

Harald acted on all three in the moments after *Runeclaw*'s crash. The gunship hit with brutal impact, but there was no time to recover. Anger gave him the impetus to leap to war. Most of his Wolf Guard had survived. So had their mounts. They battered their way out of the ruin.

Instinct had him lead his brothers to the side of the gunship facing away from the fortress walls and gun emplacements.

Runeclaw had landed on a ridge a short elevation above the battlefield. Harald followed reason and climbed onto the roof to see the extent of the disaster. Instinct again granted him speed. He was exposed for a few seconds only, and they were enough. What he saw made the anger burn ever higher.

Reason held him back from pointless recklessness.

Instead, he saw the need for the meaningful kind.

The Deathwolves had lost the coherence of any formation. They were in scattered squads at best. Some fought on their own, the only survivors of the drop pods destroyed in mid-flight. He saw two other things, which his reason seized upon.

He saw the enemy. There were Khornate daemons, but it was not those fiends who held the redoubts and turned their huge batteries on the Deathwolves. It was not daemons who had concealed the energy signatures of the defences. The enemy who used human weapons was on the field now, picking off the individual Space Wolves, eroding the strength of Whitestalker. Mobs of mortal cultists were loose upon the glacier, harassing Wulfen and Deathwolves. They were the thralls of vicious masters in horned, distorted power armour. The Traitors were clad in blue and green.

Alpha Legion.

Traitors and worse than traitors. Beings so consumed by deception there was nothing left. They defiled the honesty of war.

He felt the revulsion, the hatred. Instinct and anger sought to hurl him roaring from the roof. Reason prevailed. And it was thanks to reason he understood the other crucial sight: another stricken Stormwolf streaking overhead, its engines burning. It left a contrail of black smoke as it came in at an angle over the battlefield, overshooting Morkai's Keep. Harald made out its markings. It was *Sigurd's Might*, carrying Feingar's Coldeyes, one of the packs of Wolf Scouts.

The gunship disappeared beyond the fortress. Harald dropped

down from *Runeclaw*'s roof. As he leapt onto Icetooth's back, he pictured the geography of the glacial mesa. The fortress did not rise from the centre of the plateau. It was built at the edge of the glacier's flank. Where *Sigurd's Might* had gone down, there was only the greater drop to the wastes below.

Unless...

There was an ice ledge that jutted out partway down the ice cliff. If fate had smiled and the gunship had come to rest there...

Harald switched the vox to a private channel. 'Feingar,' he said.

In the background, he heard groaning metal. Then Feingar said, 'Yes, Lord Deathwolf.' His voice was calm, assured. The voice of a warrior who knew exactly what his task was. 'We have already begun.'

'Good,' Harald said and ended the communication.

The Thunderwolves awaited his orders. He said nothing about Feingar. The Alpha Legion were masters of misdirection and deception. To deceive them, there could be no communication with the Coldeyes. He had to keep the knowledge of what might happen from all. Even from himself, if he could.

Meaningful recklessness.

'We storm the gates,' he told the Thunderwolves. 'Take the field, and call our brothers to us. We will gather our strength once more, and our hammer will batter the foe to extinction.'

Do not think about Feingar, he told himself. Do not speculate. Ride to destroy the Traitors. Let it suffice, and it will do more than that.

He turned Icetooth and charged down the slope from *Runeclaw*. Canis and the others followed. They joined in his war cry. The wolves bayed, as enraged as their riders.

Harald rode hard for the centre of the plain. Turrets turned his way. Shells chewed up the glacier, stitching a line of craters as they sought the Thunderwolves. Ice exploded in dagger shards. But Harald's pack was fast. It defied the gunners and barrelled towards the Traitors. The shelling veered away towards other targets, avoiding the new masters of Frostheim.

The Thunderwolves fell upon a squad of Alpha Legion warriors who had surrounded a wrecked drop pod. They were pouring bolter fire into three Grey Hunters struggling from the ruin. The Space Wolves still fought, but their wounds were crippling. Two more of their brothers lay motionless beside them, their blood staining the ice crimson. The clamour of the shells covered the approach of the Thunderwolves. One of the Traitors turned at the last moment and received Glacius full in his helm's grille. Harald's strength and Ice-tooth's speed drove the blade through the armour and out the back of the Traitor's skull.

The Thunderwolves cut through the squad's line, killing three upon the instant. They turned and circled the others, strafing them with bolt pistols. The Alpha Legionnaires were caught between the fire of the riders and their former victims. They fought back with bolters millennia old. At the sight of the archaic models, Harald thought again of the Wulfen's ancient weaponry. His mind saw dark connections to be made, but he rejected them for now. All that mattered was to kill and to fight on.

As the Thunderwolves cut down the squad, the battlefield responded. Using his peripheral vision, Harald saw many brothers struggling to converge on his position. The Wulfen fought with blind rage. There was no order there.

Not all Deathwolves were making for him. Lone figures loped across the ice, howling and changing, consumed by the curse.

So many dead. So many transformed.

He rounded on the Alpha Legion with renewed fury. He let his anger strike for him. He did not let it become him. His anger was human, and so it must remain.

As the last of the Traitors went down, Harald turned to find the next kill. It found him instead. With autocannons blasting, a daemon engine emerged from behind the ruins of the drop pod. The round-bodied monster walked on two legs, had arms and a thing that might have been a head – Harald could not imagine what machine it might once have been before corruption and possession had transformed it. Now it was walking destruction, a thing with the drake's maw and autocannon limbs. The head dug its teeth into the buckled hatch of the pod and tore off a chunk of metal as if it were flesh, before devouring it. At the same time, its arms opened fire. Shells of phosphor blazed across the ice and into the Thunderwolves. Brother Onarr and his wolf blew apart. The flaming remains pattered down to the glacier. Harald and Icetooth tore through the falling flames, heading down and left, towards the other side of the drop pod.

The dire engine devoured more wreckage, then took a heavy step forward. Its feet punched deep holes into the ice and the surface melted from the monster's infernal heat. It did not let up in its fire, turning the area around the drop pod into a storm of phosphor and exploding ice. The Grey Hunters saw their rescue turn to their destruction. They turned their guns on the monster. It turned its attention to them. They disappeared in the hail of autocannon shells, their armour vaporised.

Harald rounded the drop pod and came up behind the beast, leaping from Icetooth and landing on the engine's back. The monster's carapace was a heavily shielded sphere. The beast responded to his presence by turning sharply to the left and the right, trying to shake him off. Harald hung on, grasping the grille of one of the vents. A searing wind blew from the internal furnace, scorching his face. The monster's arms and neck flailed, but Harald was out of their reach. He lunged forwards and grabbed hold of the edge of the carapace from where the plated, articulated neck emerged.

The other Thunderwolves circled the engine. Two more packs had joined the fight and their bolt pistol fire hammered against the carapace. The explosive shells did no more than crack the surface. The fiend stamped and roared, firing in a circle. Incandescent death pursued the Thunderwolves. It found two more.

Cursing, Harald held on to the carapace with his left hand and, with his right, he pulled krak grenades from his belt. He thrust them into the join between the neck and body, fixing four grenades to the beast, clustering them on the same point. Then he jumped away from it.

He landed on his feet. He was inside the circle of the monster's fire. Its blind maw craned down at him, inorganic teeth snapping.

The grenades went off, one after the other, melting through the plates of the neck, tearing open the beast, reaching its burning core. A geyser of flames shot out from the base of the neck. The daemonic engine staggered. A machinic scream of pain tore itself from its throat. Its autocannons fell silent. Then it fired again, without a target now, blasting at the entire world in its agony. The shells were of its body, and it consumed itself in its pain. The fire jetted higher, pushing the wound wider, until the monster cracked in half. Harald shielded his gaze from the searing light. The beast disappeared into its own pyre.

Icetooth bounded over the crevasses opened by the shells. Harald climbed onto his back once more. He led the charge anew. There could not be pause, no chance for the turrets to acquire the Thunderwolves as targets.

Harald became the gravitational pull of the battlefield. Riding down the centre of the glacier towards the gates, he was visible to all, and he pulled his scattered brothers towards him. The enemy sought to block their gathering, the keep's batteries and daemonic cannons smashing Deathwolves to pulp and ashes. Cultists swarmed over them. Traitors picked off lone figures with cold precision, but they too were caught by the gravity. They responded to the threat of the Thunderwolves, and closed in.

The Wulfen and the Deathwolves who had fallen to the curse were nearer too. They followed the path of frenzy. It led them to the groupings of prey.

Batteries on the left and right converged fire, two gatling cannons and a battle cannon creating an impassable curtain of shredding, pounding shells before the gates of Morkai's Keep. There was the line, Harald knew. If the Thunderwolves reached that point, they would go no further. Even so, he urged Icetooth to run faster. Keep up the pressure, he thought. Keep the enemy's focus.

He had stolen the battle's momentum from the Alpha Legion, despite their massive advantage in armament and position. The advantage was temporary. The Alpha Legion had time. Stalemate would result in the Traitors' victory.

Meaningful recklessness, he thought. And so he led the charge as if the artillery barrage meant nothing.

There were enemies still to kill before the terminal point. Ahead of him was a band of elite Traitors butchering Long Fangs. Off to the right, a lone Alpha Legion warrior moved through the struggling Deathwolves like a serpent of lightning. He was a blur. In the rush of his own speed, Harald could not catch more than a brief glimpse of the warrior. He left a wake of blood, Grey Hunters and Blood Claws falling to his assault. A handful of Wulfen and Blood Claws, enraged by this viper of war, abandoned the effort to reach their Wolf Lord and turned on the nearer foe. Turret fire dogged their movements. They were wounded and slowing as they tried to surround the Traitor. He welcomed them to their end. Harald saw the circle tighten. He looked away at the nearer band of Traitors, coming into reach within seconds. When he checked again, severed heads lay on the glacier. Only two Wulfen still fought, and one had lost an arm.

The sight of that single killer spiked Harald's rage. There, he was certain, was the lord of the Traitors, and the cause of Frostheim's suffering. Harald's rage urged him to turn Icetooth from his path and hunt the warlord down.

Reason held him back.

His place was before the gates. There were more of his brothers fighting their last here. And these Traitors were closer.

'Fenris!' Harald roared as the Thunderwolves raced through explosions of ice shards. He pulled Glacius back, preparing to pay the Alpha Legionnaires in kind and decapitate the first warrior in his path.

He swung. The axe blade whistled through empty air. His target had moved with sinuous grace. The entire band shifted their focus as if the Thunderwolves had been their goal all along, and the Long Fangs merely bait. Harald's foe was suddenly at Icetooth's left flank. His bolt pistol cracked. Shells slammed into Harald's shoulder plate and ceramite splintered. The impact knocked him from Icetooth and onto his back. A Traitor aimed a power sword at his neck, the weapon flashing with wyrd energy, but Harald rolled to his right, firing his bolt pistol to the left. The glacier hissed where the sword struck. There was no sound of his shots finding their mark. He leapt to his feet and the sword was in front of him, plunging towards his chest. He knocked it aside and sidestepped, and a bolt shell exploded against his left shoulder.

A sudden fog surrounded him. It was a smear of jagged black and white. He could not be sure how many Traitors he fought. They moved like a single being, one opponent always in his weak spot. From some unknowable distance, he heard Canis call his name, then snarl. Weapons clashed on all sides, invisible beyond the wall. The sword, one or many, stabbed and slashed. He blocked most of the strikes, but the Traitor, one or many, had the advantage of speed. Blows hit home, cutting through the seams of his armour. When he struck back with Glacius and bolt pistol, he attacked nothing but air.

One or many, they were wearing him down.

In the distance, a bellow of pain that descended to a gurgle.

Feingar, make your move, he willed.

A blinding flash of energy. Silver pain sinking between his ribs.

Feingar, we are out of time.

CHAPTER 8

Ritual's End

Flies.

Flies and blood.

Blood and change.

Change and pain.

The daemons' gifts to the mortal realm filled Deepspark. Four princes of Chaos marched to war, and there was no aspect of the cavern that was not one with their corruption. The floors of the walkways squirmed and bit. The rails rotted and burst with sprays of venomous spores. The walls of hab-huts ran with smoking blood. Death sang its music of seduction, inviting the mind to the contemplation of the sensuousness of blood, the decadence of severed limbs, the headiness of butchered meat.

And in the midst of the manifold tortures of corruption, there was the gift. The purity of the hunting animal. The total abandon of bloodletting, yet bloodletting not without purpose. Threats must be extinguished. Prey must be run to ground. There was no corrupt pleasure in the kill. There was no shrieking, mindless vengeance. There was necessity. There was instinct.

The arm of the warrior and the fury of the beast.

Ulrik saw and understood all this. The war in Deepspark was an avalanche of sensation and revelation. He fought through walls of daemonic flesh. His body acted on instinct so rapid and urgent that his mind barely registered his actions. In his left hand, his plasma pistol fired and fired and fired, the rhythm of the bursts stopping just short of the critical overheating – blast after blast of destructive light, incinerating the skulls of abominations, melting their torsos. His crozius smashed form and devastated flesh. Plague daemons, Khornate swordlings, the clawed dancers of Slaanesh and the pink nightmares of Tzeentch pressed in on him, struggling against each other to strike the killing blow. He waded deeper and deeper, cursing them in the name of Fenris and its spirits. His voice was raw with the power of his anger.

He bellowed, though he did not hear his own words. No speech could be heard over the fire of storm bolters and white-noise roar of flamers, echoing and building against the cavern walls. Ulrik reacted to the daemonic strikes, countering them and retaliating with killing force, yet the eyes of his spirit looked past the immediate foe. His struggle was to reach the daemon prince ahead of him. It was the one embraced by the runic, soundless cry of Tzen'char. It had a form. It was winged. It had limbs. It towered over the lesser daemons of its horde. But its form seemed contingent on the whims of its will and the moment. Its movements had a swift, stuttering quality, as if fragments of time kept falling away. Its arm was raised, and then its talons were impaling one of the Wulfen without it ever bringing the arm down. As Ulrik drew nearer to its position on the platform, he saw an impossible depth to the daemon's shape. To stare into its being was to see an existence stretching far beyond this place and time. The depths twisted and coiled and branched. Each flicker of its being brought a different version of the daemon from elsewhere. The closer Ulrik came, the more he had a sense he was approaching an incarnated labyrinth.

He had to reach the daemon. He had to fight alongside the Wulfen,

who had surrounded the abomination. This struggle was a fulfilment of destiny. This was what the Wulfen had returned to fight.
The gift of their bestial fury was the answer to the curse of the daemons. They had clawed their way through and over the lesser foes,
straight to the creators of the madness.

And they were being cut down.

No, Ulrik thought. No.

He would not let them fall. He howled, and the beast raced
through his veins. He would tear through the abomination before
him with his bare hands.

At his shoulder was an even greater roar. Logan Grimnar barrelled
into the horde. His face was contorted. His eyes were red and blazing. His fangs were bared.

The way forward became clear to Ulrik. The frenzy of the Wulfen
must not be contained, but embraced and channelled. It was
spreading now, and it would destroy the abominations before them.
It would be Midgardia's salvation.

Ulrik's howl became a cry of savage joy.

The blow hit the side of his head. It was so powerful it seemed
to strike his entire frame. It knocked him to the floor of the platform. He fell on his back and darkness crept in at the edges of his
vision. It withdrew, but the cavern spun. His limbs did not obey
his commands.

The daemon prince of Nurgle loomed over him. Beneath a face-
plate, its mouth gaped in a leprous, contemptuous grin. Flies poured
out from beneath its teeth. It lurched away from him, its jaw unhing-
ing to spew a vast swarm of insects over the Space Wolves.

Ulrik struggled to clear his vision. Feeling was returning too slowly
to his arms and legs. The blow from Mordokh had been more than
physical.

Rise. Rise and hunt.

The beast gave him strength. He started to move. He still could
not see clearly. The war was a dizzying vortex. The platform rocked
and suspension cables parted with a vicious twang and a walkway

covered in struggling Space Wolves and daemons fell to the lava below.

A lithe, reptilian presence stood over him. The Slaaneshi prince held the eyes of Ulrik's brothers in one hand. It reached towards his helm with the other.

And then its face split in half. The Axe Morkai was deep in its skull.

Grimnar, baying his wrath, struck faster than Ulrik had ever seen. He moved with the speed of the unleashed predator.

The change was taking hold.

Rise.

Hunt.

Ulrik snarled. Crimson fury flooded his mind. He lurched to his feet. His vision at last began to clear, and Grimnar had already moved to a new target. Malyg'nyl was on its knees, elegant claws struggling to hold its head together. The Khornate Prince Arkh'gar clashed with Grimnar. Already the daemon was bleeding.

Yes, Ulrik thought. He staggered forward to the Great Wolf's aid. The gift takes us to victory. 'We will open the way for Russ!' he shouted. 'We shall–'

Laughter cut through his words. Tzen'char spread its wings. It spoke a sentence that flickered and looped through the labyrinths of existence and madness as the daemon's form did. A scream of the immaterium howled from the centre of the cavern. A flash of unlight cut through Ulrik's armour and slashed his flesh. Bleeding from a hundred cuts, he kept his feet. He blinked his eyes clear.

The daemons were gone.

On the platform and walkways, Terminators and Wulfen stopped in mid-strike.

The shriek of the wyrd passed. It was replaced by the rumbling crack of stone. The walls and ceiling of the cavern split. A web of crevasses spread and joined. All of Deepspark shook as the end approached.

Ulrik howled his denial. But the wounded, weakened body of

Midgardia did not care for prophecy. The cracks built to thunder, the thunder to a mountain's roar, and then everything fell.

Fell into the crushing dark.

A shape ripped through the fog.

Massive. A thing of sinew and claws and fangs.

A monster of the bloody past and of the uncertain future.

Yngvir slammed an Alpha Legionnaire to the ground. He stood on the Traitor's back and seized his helm then twisted and yanked back, tearing off the Traitor's head. He held his trophy high, blood raining down upon him, and howled.

The fog began to break up. Yngvir lashed out into the fading limbo, and suddenly he was holding another enemy by the arm. The Traitor turned his blade against Yngvir. The Wulfen was the equal in speed to the Traitor. With the fluidity of the perfect kill, he released the Traitor, evaded the blow, and countered with his relic frost claws. He struck with both arms, shattering the Alpha Legionnaire's armour and plunging the huge blades through the Traitor's carapace and into his hearts.

Now the fog was gone. So was the intricate, interlocking choreography of battle that had turned the band of warriors into a single being. Yngvir had broken their unity. Harald struck, and this time he found his target. Glacius severed the sword arm of the warrior before him. The Traitor stumbled back, spraying blood. He raised his bolt pistol. Harald plunged his axe blade through the Traitor's chest.

Around him, the Thunderwolf cavalry brought down the enemy with the full savagery of vengeance. Every blow Harald landed had a richly satisfying impact.

And all the time he thought, three times. Yngvir had saved his life three times. He owed a transcendent debt of honour to the warrior he believed to be cursed.

An explosion shook the upper levels of Morkai's Keep. Armourglass blew outward. The turrets fell silent. At last, Harald heard

Feingar's voice on the vox once more. *'The Keep is ours, Lord Deathwolf.'*

Harald stood back from an Alpha Legion corpse. He yanked Glacius from the skull. He looked over the battlefield.

'Your Scouts have given us victory,' he told Feingar.

The elite Traitors were slaughtered. With the artillery down, the superior numbers of the Deathwolves were now turning the tide. A new inevitability had come to the glacier. Harald pushed aside the thought of how many brothers had been lost. There would be time to mourn and celebrate their sagas when the war was won.

He looked for the Alpha Legion warlord. There, a few hundred metres away. He had lost the purpose in his movements. He hesitated, motionless in the midst of the battlefield's eddying smoke.

Are you wondering what has happened to your guns? Harald thought. He pounded across the glacier towards the warlord. *Are you wondering what happened to your victory?*

The warlord's hesitation was fatal. He was a motionless target. He did not see the enormous silhouette close in on him through the smoke. Icetooth slammed into the Traitor with the force of a tank. The warlord fell, rose again to defend himself, managing to strike the thunderwolf once before Icetooth brought him down with finality. The crack of a snapping spine sounded over the glacier.

Icetooth stood guard over his prey until Harald arrived. The Traitor reached for his lost sword, but he was broken. He could not move. He looked up at Harald. 'The ritual is complete, lapdog,' he said. 'Killing me won't change anything.' Empty insults, empty defiance. The Traitor sought some shred of pride, some measure of dignity at his end.

Harald granted him neither. 'Maybe not, but it'll make me feel better.' With a single blow from Glacius, he decapitated the Alpha Legionnaire.

Harald kicked the head away from the twitching body. He had not lied – the execution was satisfying. It did make him feel better.

Then he looked out across the glacier, at the blood and the cost, at the rampaging Wulfen, and at his transformed brothers. He thought about his debt to Yngvir, and of the contagion that had shut down strategic thinking.

Damnation and salvation. He did not know how to separate them. Or if there was still time to do so.

The three Stormwolves flew through the tumbling wreckage of the Grey Knights vessel. As they angled towards the surface of Valdrmani and made for Longhowl, chunks of the battle-barge became a hard rain upon the moon. There were few remains of any size. Compared to the vessel that had been, Krom was passing through the ashes of cremation.

On the bridge of the *Winterbite*, he had seen the ruby streak of the nova cannon shot, the flash. By the time the frigate had reached the far side of Valdrmani, the fires had faded. There had been nothing but the night of the void, the ashes, and the terrible absence.

Too late, he had thought. Too late. You held true to your oath too long.

Then the augur array had detected the fading signature of engines on the surface of the moon.

The Stormwolves flew close to the domes and passed over the landing site of the Stormravens. The gunships were intact.

'Smoke rises from the main gates,' said Hrothgar, looking through the viewing block.

'A good sign,' Krom said. 'They went in fighting.'

The Iron Priest gestured at the domeplex. 'A big area to search.'

Krom nodded. 'We'll make for the nova cannon emplacement. We can start there. I would want vengeance for my ship.'

'Aye,' said Hrothgar.

'*Lord Dragongaze,*' Egil Redfist voxed from his Stormwolf. '*Bolter flashes three hundred metres to port.*'

Krom had been focusing on the column of the cannon. He looked down in the direction Redfist had indicated. The Blood Claw leader was right – a spot midway down the height of the dome strobed with the distinctive lightning burst of gunfire.

'Take us there,' he ordered.

The squadron dropped, closing in until it was flying almost flush with the anti-rad crystalglass skin of the dome. The interior of Long-howl was lit with a sick glow that pulsed slowly from red to green to bone-grey. Monstrous shadows cavorted. They grew in number the closer the gunships came to the flashes.

'Good,' Krom said when they reached the position. The word felt strange to utter. When had he last been able to look at anything and declare it *good?* He had just passed through the dust of a Grey Knights battle-barge. He beheld the settlement of Fenris' moon overrun by daemons. And now he saw a small band of Grey Knights surrounded by daemons led by a bloodthirster. The Grey Knights were moments from being overwhelmed. Even so, Krom said, 'Good.' The battle was not over.

There was still time.

'On my signal,' Krom voxed to all three Stormwolves, 'breach the dome.' Over an open channel, he broadcast, 'Grey Knights! Incoming! Brace!' Then he said, '*Now.*'

Skyhammer missiles and lascannons struck the dome. The battle flashes vanished behind the greater blaze of explosions and the dome wall burst outwards, turned to powder in the violent decompression. The atmosphere of the dome rushed out, carrying with it the daemonic horde. Las and twin-linked heavy bolters pulverised the enemy cloud. More missiles streaked towards the bloodthirster as it sailed out, carried by a wind more powerful than its wings. It disappeared in the multiple blast.

'Take us in,' Krom said when the last of the daemons were scattered over the surface of Valdrmani.

The three Stormwolves flew in through the huge breach. Their assault ramps dropped before they had finished settling. Krom strode down first. His Fierce-eye's Finest followed.

The Wulfen came last.

The Grey Knights said nothing but headed for the nearest exit from the void-struck quadrant of the dome. Even when both armed parties were on the other side of a sealed bulkhead and in a full atmosphere again, they remained silent. Krom eyed them and their captain. He could list a dozen reasons effortlessly why he had contempt for their order, but their actual presence was impressive. It was more than the superlative Aegis armour and the perfection of the Nemesis power weapons. The cold nobility commanded respect.

Krom felt the strength of the captain's gaze even beneath the Grey Knight's helmet. When the captain's attention passed from Krom to the Wulfen, Krom chose that moment to laugh.

'You can embarrass us with thanks a bit later,' he said. 'Once our work is done. I am Krom Dragongaze, Wolf Lord of the Drakeslayers. My men and I are honoured to fight at your side.'

The Grey Knight captain looked a few moments longer at the Wulfen. Serkir held them in order. Low growls issued from their throats, but their attention was focused beyond the Grey Knights. The captain faced Krom.

'Brother-Captain Stern of the Third Brotherhood,' he said, and held out his hand. Krom did the same. They clasped forearms.

'We have to move quickly,' Stern said. 'Whatever the daemons are doing, it is almost done.'

As the tension of the immediate moment passed, Krom noticed the growing pressure behind his eyes. It throbbed with the pulsing of the unnatural light. 'There is something...' he began.

'Yes,' said Stern. 'You feel it, then. There is a ritual at work on this moon.'

There were two exits from the storage bay in which the Fierce-eyes and the Grey Knights found themselves. Stern headed for the one on the left.

'What sort of ritual?' Krom asked. He signalled for his warriors to follow. The Grey Knights had fought their way this far. They would have done so for a good reason.

'I do not know, as yet. I believe the destruction of our vessel is part of its work, however. Every event since the formation of the warp storms has been part of a foul pattern. The ritual is reaching the critical point. We cannot permit its completion.'

'How do you know this? Or that we must go in this direction?'

'Are you a psyker, Lord Dragongaze?'

'I am not!' He made a sign of maleficarum.

'Yet you can feel the energy. Imagine, then, my experience of it.'

Time, Krom thought. In the end, there was even less than he had dreaded.

Lord Skayle had fallen silent.

In the astropathic choristrium of Longhowl's command sanctum, Hekastis Nul walked the circumference of the glyph, musing about the silence. The Dark Apostle felt little concern. It did not matter to him whether Skayle lived or died. Nul would be dead himself in a few minutes. But his anticipation of the great moment was acute, and his preparations were complete. He filled the remaining seconds by contemplating the implications of his lord's defeat. Perhaps the Dogs had reclaimed Frostheim. Maybe Svellgard too, or at least established a foothold there. Unless they had performed Exterminatus on their own moon, it was impossible that they should have banished millions of daemons in so short a time.

'Did you lose Frostheim, Lord Skayle?' Nul mused aloud.

Standing around the glyph, his cultists bore witness as it approached its great flowering. The astropaths of Longhowl were alive, after a fashion, but they no longer had flesh or minds. Imprisoned in their cradles, their power, their pain, their sanity and their selves had been siphoned into the glyph. They were melted, deformed figures, still convulsing in agony, still screaming, kept alive by the hunger of the thing they were feeding.

'If the Dogs have Frostheim,' Nul reasoned, 'they now have hope. If they have hope, what follows will be richer still. Therefore, Lord Skayle, your death is part of our pattern.'

The power in the choristrium spiked. So did Nul's anticipation.

He stopped pacing and looked at the glyph, standing between two of his cultists.

The glyph was daubed in daemons' blood. It occupied the centre of the choristrium, embracing the astropathic cradles. Its light was as painful to behold as a sun's. The light in the chamber had ceased to shift colours. Now it was a jade of mind-stabbing intensity. Soon the glyph would bring about an apotheosis of pain, and with it, the end of the Space Wolves. The blast that would destroy Longhowl and all within was no more than a by-product of its true goal.

The goal was the vision – the vision that would travel across the galaxy. The vision of Grey Knights murdered by the Space Wolves. The vision for the entire Imperium.

The final moments slipped away. As they did, the Dark Apostle felt another tension begin to fold and cut the air. A being that was many and one was coming from many directions and none. The Living Labyrinth approached.

Nul said, 'I am glad, master, you have chosen to witness the moment.'

On the other side of the choristrium, his wards at the entrance collapsed, banished. Their sudden release of energy blew the doors apart. Shredded metal flew across the dome. The dogs who did not understand they were already dead rushed in.

You are too late. I will show you.

Hekastis Nul stepped into the glyph.

Energies erupted around him.

Beyond the doorway, Krom saw the fate of his Chapter reduced to seconds. He charged into the chamber. By his oath, he would prove those seconds to be enough.

'*Cultists!*' Stern voxed. '*In cover behind the cradles.*'

'Petty little men,' said Krom as lasgun fire streaked his way. 'Drakeslayers!' he called. 'Put them down!'

The Space Wolves spread out through the room. Their fire wreaked monstrous havoc on the mortals. The cultists were armed, and shot back, but the effort was futile. They did nothing to slow their execution.

'Kill them all and kill them now!' Krom ordered. Faster, he thought. Faster. He streaked around the circumference of the chamber, his axe cutting down another cultist with every step. He was a scythe. He fired into the cradles as he ran, killing the astropaths too. His one thought was to stop the energy flow into the glyph.

'Commendable vehemence,' said Stern. *'Lord Krom, keep them busy. My warriors and I will finish this. Brothers! The Rite of Nullification!'*

The Wulfen and the Fierce-eye's Finest hit the humans of the choristrium like a cyclone of bolter shells and blades. The air filled with a deluge of blood, but the energy was still building. Green light lashed out from the centre of the glyph. The pressure was so intense, Krom's ears began to bleed. The dome of the choristrium cracked. The walls and floor vibrated, on the verge of shattering outward. The seconds were falling away to nothing.

The Grey Knights began their counter-ritual, moving into the glyph. Hurry, Krom thought, glancing away from the killing to see their progress. They were moving with deliberation, marching directly into the blazing energy, pushing against it. The wyrd lashed out. It could not keep them away.

Hurry, Krom willed. There is no time.

There was a concussion at the centre of the glyph. For a moment, Krom thought the end had come, but it had not. The pressure still mounted. The light strobed with madness and shrieked with rage. From its blinding core came a Dark Apostle of the Alpha Legion.

Stern plunged into battle with the Traitor.

Krom was less than a quarter of the way through his run of butchery. There were hundreds of cultists, scores of astropaths. His warrior blood cried out to attack the Traitor, but he did not. His oath had kept him inactive on Fenris so he might be here, now, at this most critical juncture. His duty to Fenris now was massacre.

Even the Wulfen did not turn to the greater prey. They understood.

Without the energy from the cultists and the astropaths, the Dark Apostle was a single figure, all but powerless.

Drain the glyph.

So much blood. So many mortals dead now, and yes, the terrible light wavered. The rhythm of the searing pulses of jade light slowed. It became syncopated. The light began to fade.

Now the last of the cultists was cut down, and the cradles of the astropaths were all destroyed. The Dark Apostle was on his knees, impaled by Stern's sword. He was shouting. He shrieked the name Tzen'char. The sound of the name hurt Krom's eyes.

But the light was fading. The light was...

No...

No!

The energy built once more, faster and more terrible than before. More than blinding. The dome of the choristrium seemed to melt and shake at once. Reality tore, and the chamber filled with daemons. The air around the contours of the glyph vomited into existence pink horrors and flame daemons by the hundreds. A firestorm of wyrdflame hit the Space Wolves. Blood Claws turned to glass and shattered. Wulfen were devoured by new maws on their own bodies. The daemons fell on the Grey Knights, disrupting the counter-ritual. The Grey Knights cut down the abominations as fast as they attacked, but they attacked without cease. The flood would come until the purpose of the glyph was fulfilled.

The blast was imminent. Krom's mind filled with jagged fragments of betrayal and mutation.

The wyrd roared with awful birth, and the dread owner of the name howled by the Dark Apostle appeared. It stood before Krom at the edge of the glyph. Majestic in triumph, Tzen'char spread its wings.

'*Stern!*' it roared. The Grey Knight looked up.

Krom charged at the daemon. He rammed his shoulder into the abomination's back. It was like running headlong into a mountainside. The impact stunned him, but the daemon fell. He emptied his bolt pistol into its skull. Suddenly he was staring at the front of the daemon. The maze of its being reassembled its configuration in the blink of an eye. It was prone, and then it was standing, and its sword had pierced Krom's left shoulder. His pistol arm went numb. He stepped forward into the blade, moving to within striking distance again, raising his axe.

The daemon laughed. It raised its right hand. Energy danced from the claws, as blinding as the unholy light of the glyph.

Serkir leapt at Tzen'char. His frost axe came down on that right arm. It bit deep. The labyrinthine being shifted again. Serkir's blade went all the way through and struck the floor. The daemon's arm was untouched. Serkir's attack had gained Krom one second more of life.

And the daemon laughed. The sorcery on its talons became a roaring nimbus as it reached for Krom.

He could see nothing except the light. The burning, destroying light.

Except now the light was filled with prayer. And the daemon was screaming.

The malignant jade shattered, replaced by the purity of silver.

The energy of the wyrd came apart, broken from the inside. Stern was there. Stern had entered the eye of the wyrdstorm. Krom had turned the daemon's attention away, and the Grey Knight had stabbed his holy sword into the centre of the glyph.

Tzen'char screamed. All the daemons screamed.

The build-up of energy was reversed. Even the glyph shrieked.

The light of judgement consumed all that was unholy.

EPILOGUE

It had been Scout Dolutas, wounded almost to death by the savagery of mutated Space Wolves. It had not even had to speak to deliver its message to Araphil, to give him the answers he dreaded. The Dark Angels had seen the images held by the skull. They had been reluctant to draw the terrible conclusions, but their thoughts had been inexorably pulled towards that chasm. They had taken the bait, and the great event had begun.

It had been Master Astropath Asconditus. Into Sammael's ears it had delivered questions and suspicions, all constructed around the tiny fragments of another lie. It rejoiced in the perfection of its art as Sammael, reluctantly, slowly, but inevitably, had walked still further down the path.

Then that form of Asconditus had served its purpose too. Another kill, another disappearance on the Rock. The little touches gave it so much pleasure. It watched the Dark Angels begin to suspect an alliance between the Space Wolves and a daemonic party. It tried to remember when it had last tasted such delight.

Now it was the seneschal Vox Mendaxis, and it waited upon Grand

Master Azrael. Events were proceeding so perfectly, it had no need to act for the moment. There were no messages to twist. No orders to misinterpret. Azrael had the facts: Chaos taint in the entire Fenris system, Space Wolves transforming into Wulfen. Nothing but the truth.

Azrael was still regrettably hesitant. For the moment, though. Only for the moment.

Under the hood of Vox Mendaxis, the Changeling suppressed a smile.

The vox system was working again in the damaged command centre of Morkai's Keep. The unit was a powerful one, and some of the interference had diminished. Harald established contact with Sven Bloodhowl, holding the World Wolf's Lair on Svellgard. The Iron Priests of both companies used the signals from the two fortresses to amplify each other.

And now he heard Krom Dragongaze's voice, too.

Harald stood at the gaping hole in the command centre's wall. He looked up into the night sky of Frostheim while he spoke to Dragongaze.

'Brother,' he said, 'it is good to speak to you.'

'*And you. What news of the Great Wolf?*'

'None. Communication with Lord Iron Wolf has been fragmentary. The situation on Midgardia is dire. All contact with Grimnar's strike force has ceased.' He paused. 'The Iron Wolf says there was an earthquake...'

'*I will not believe it,*' said Dragongaze. '*We have hope now. Let us use it well. We purged Valdrmani. We will free our other worlds too.*'

At the augur bank behind Harald, Feingar shouted, 'Vessels translating in-system!'

Harald rushed back inside. 'Who?' he asked.

'Dark Angels,' Feingar said. He tapped the augur network's pict screen. One reading after another appeared. 'Ultramarines. Iron Hands...' More than a dozen different Chapter runes appeared over the vessel signals. Then came those of Knightly houses. Then mass transporters of the Astra Militarum. The fleet was immense.

'Dragongaze,' Harald said, 'Are you picking up the same signatures?' He had so many doubts. There had been so much deception. He had to be sure.

'*We are,*' the Fierce-eye said. '*It looks like a substantial portion of the Dark Angels fleet before we even count the rest.*'

'It *is* their fleet,' Feingar said. Then his eyes widened. He pointed to a rune many times larger than the rest. 'Russ,' he swore. 'That's the Rock!'

Doubts. Patterns. Dooms within dooms. Harald felt the events click together like the gears of a terrible machine. As Feingar updated the positions of the fleet minute by minute, Harald returned to the breach once more. He watched the sky.

He witnessed the passage of a moon, one that did not belong in the Fenris System.

He saw the movement of stars he knew to be warships.

He was still watching when the sky flared, and the bombardment of the Fenris System began.

ABOUT THE AUTHOR

David Annandale is the author of The Horus Heresy novel *The Damnation of Pythos*. He also writes the Yarrick series, consisting of the novella *Chains of Golgotha* and the novels *Imperial Creed* and *The Pyres of Armageddon*. For Space Marine Battles he has written *The Death of Antagonis* and *Overfiend*. He is a prolific writer of short fiction, including the novella *Mephiston: Lord of Death* and numerous short stories set in The Horus Heresy and Warhammer 40,000 universes and the Age of Sigmar. David lectures at a Canadian university, on subjects ranging from English literature to horror films and video games.

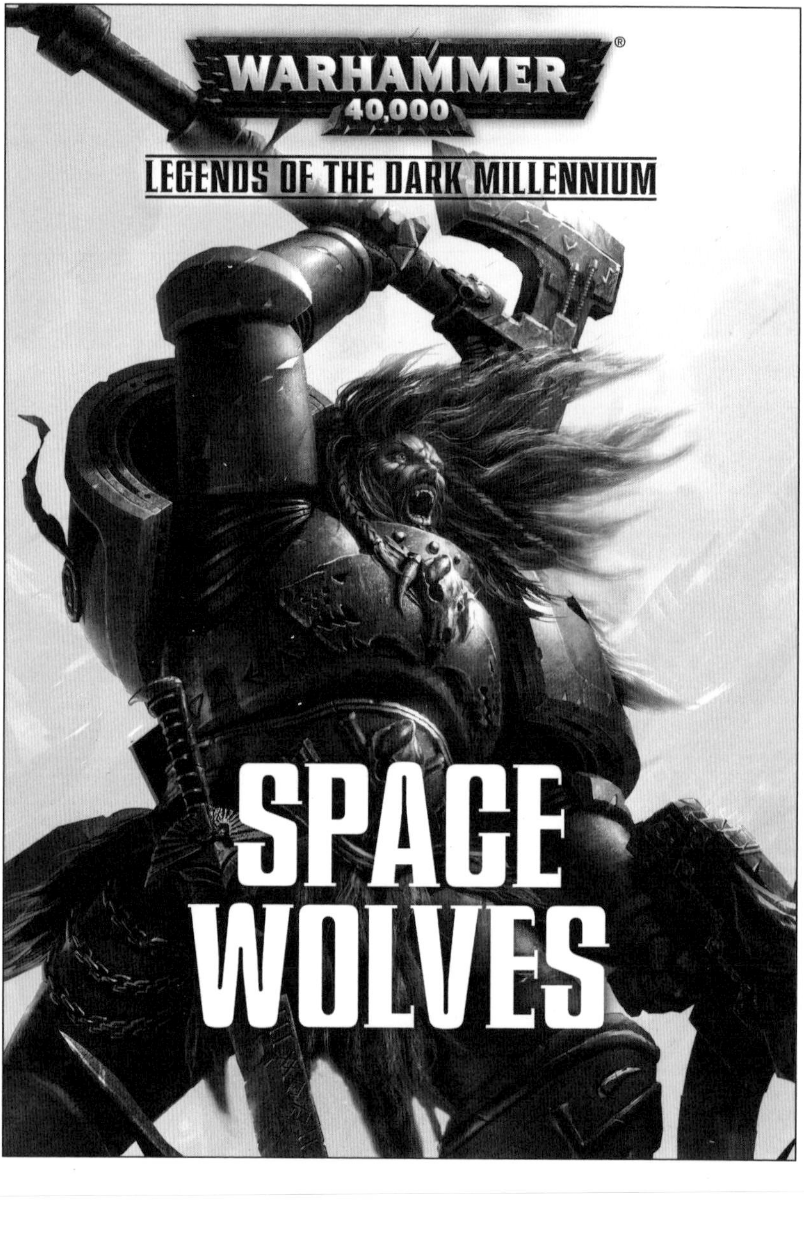
WARHAMMER
40,000
LEGENDS OF THE DARK MILLENNIUM
SPACE
WOLVES

An extract from *Feast of Lies* by Ben Counter,
taken from the Legends of the Dark Millenium

SPACE WOLVES

For the first time in many years, Logan Grimnar was exhausted from battle. He had held off the tau for nearly three days as the xenos had sent unending packs of attack-beasts and swift hover-tanks to harass the Space Wolves.

The aliens had paid dearly for the chance to tire out the Great Wolf of Fenris. Hundreds of tau and their alien auxiliaries lay among the rocky canyons covering the surface of Dactyla. Now, as the Great Company faced the xenos outside, Grimnar stood on the threshold of the temple he had come to this world to find.

'Can the Great Company stand?' asked one of Grimnar's champions. Each of the half-dozen warriors was taken from the Chapter's Wolf Guard, armed with Terminator armour and their pick of weaponry from the Fang's armoury. It was rare that anyone would speak to Grimnar so bluntly, and Grimnar still had ample fury in him to round on the warrior.

'You know better than to question the resolve of our brethren,' he snarled. 'They will stand as long as they have to. And we will ensure that is not for long. Follow me and speak no more.'

The temple was more ancient than the Great Crusade itself. Echoes of a long-dead xenos empire's architecture broke through the living rock of the tunnel complex beneath the ground. Even as Grimnar led his champions down further, he could hear the reports of tau pulse rifles and the replying volleys of bolter fire.

They were Space Wolves, and the tau were as drained by the running battle as Grimnar and his brethren were. The Great Company would hold. The tau assault would be blunted. He knew this because this was the place the runes had described, and Grimnar would not return from this hunt empty-handed.

'There,' said Grimnar, indicating a symbol cut into the wall. It resembled a serpent coiling around a skull. 'Njal Stormcaller cast that rune as I watched. We are close. Just a little further.'

Grimnar felt the weight of the Axe Morkai as he walked. The warrior he had once been would have dearly loved to lay it down and rest, but those were the thoughts of a lazy pup and not the Great Wolf, so he forged on until he came upon a massive circular slab of rock blocking the way ahead.

Without a word, Grimnar put a shoulder against the rock and pushed. The Wolf Guard joined him, adding their strength to his. The slab rolled aside, revealing the way into the chamber that lay at the heart of the complex.

Purple light bled from the vault. Grimnar's autosenses were not enough to shut down the glare completely, and he held a hand in front of his face, squinting. The Wolf Guard had their storm bolters ready to open fire on any enemy that might emerge from the temple's core, but they held their fire.

They saw what Grimnar did. And in that moment, all the weariness of battle was gone.

Ulrik's watch included the dawn hours, when the blood-red light of Fenris' sun broke across the glacier-bound mountains. It was the season of fire, when Fenris came closest to its star and the equatorial oceans boiled. In the environs of the Fang there was no warmth, but the ground heaved and cracked like distant thunder as the glaciers experienced a rare thaw.

'It will be today,' said a voice behind Ulrik. It was that of the Wolf Lord Krom Dragongaze, whose Great Company had the duty of manning the Fang during the Thirtieth Great Hunt. Krom wore his trophy rack on the back of his power armour, surrounding his ruddy face with a halo of jangling bone. The orange ridge of hair along his scalp was dark in the reddish dawn light. 'Do you not think so, Lord Slayer?'

'Perhaps,' said Ulrik. He anticipated the return of the Great Companies as much as any at the Fang, and yet he could not let the emotions of a Fenrisian close to the surface.

'I can smell it,' said Krom. 'My Great Company is restless. It is not a glorious task, to serve as housekeepers here while the rest of the Chapter is on the hunt. I must fight to keep them focused, and yet I itch to be let off the leash myself.'

'Sometimes,' said Ulrik, 'we must keep the wolf caged.'

'That is not as easy for us as it is for you,' said Krom shortly.

Ulrik kept looking into the distance. He wore, as always, his armour's skull-faced helmet, and so Krom had no chance of reading anything from his face. Ulrik let the silence fall, broken only by the distant moan of the thaw and the cries of frosthawks wheeling overhead.

'Forgive me,' said Krom. 'I spoke out of turn.'

Ulrik did not move to face the Wolf Lord, and instead pointed a finger up towards the colouring sky. A silver streak was just visible there, like a falling star, a thread of precious metal suspended.

'The *Canis Pax*,' said Ulrik. 'You were correct, Lord Dragongaze. It is today.'

SPACE MARINE BATTLES

WAR OF
THE FANG

CHRIS WRAIGHT

THE HUNT FOR MAGNUS • BATTLE OF THE FANG

READ IT FIRST

EXCLUSIVE PRODUCTS | EARLY RELEASES | FREE DELIVERY
blacklibrary.com